She gla...
what he...
wanting...

Had that k... ... ...p... their
relationship? The mere idea of that rattled her as
much as the kiss. "I don't know about you, Denver,
but I'm not really in the mood for a movie."

Braking at a stop sign, he glanced over at her. "I'm
not, either. So what would you like to do? The night
is still early."

"It's rainy and cold. Why don't we just go to my
place? I'll make us some hot chocolate and we can
watch TV—or something."

"Are you sure? If there's something else you'd rather
do, just tell me. I don't want this to be a bum date
for you."

"Just spending time with you will be special."

An odd expression flickered across his face, and for
a moment she thought he was going to insist they
do anything besides what she was suggesting.

But then he shrugged one shoulder and turned the
truck in the general direction of her house.

Marcella settled back in the seat and wondered
if she'd just invited herself a heartbreak, or finally
found the courage to open the door to the rest of
her life.

MEN OF THE WEST:
Whether ranchers or lawmen, these heartbreakers
know how to ride, shoot—and drive a woman crazy...

Dear Reader,

When my Men of the West series migrated to Carson City, Nevada, and the Silver Horn Ranch, I never expected nurses to show up. After all, these were stories about cowboys, not the health profession. But for one reason or another my characters continued to end up at Tahoe General Hospital, and the medical institution began to take on a life of its own.

Momentous occasions have certainly occurred at Tahoe General, and through the years, Nurse Marcella Grayson has watched her best friends find lasting love and give birth to their babies. As a single mother of two boys, she doesn't want to think her chances to have a husband and more children have passed, but she has her doubts. Until she meets Denver Yates, ramrod at the Silver Horn.

The dark, reserved cowboy is everything Marcella wants, but Denver's plan for the future doesn't include a wife and babies. However, Christmas is coming, and the special holiday has a way of making magical things happen.

I hope you'll travel with me once again to the high desert country of Nevada and celebrate Christmas with everyone on the Silver Horn and their friends at Tahoe General Hospital!

Happy trails and Merry Christmas!

Love,

Stella

The Cowboy's Christmas Lullaby

Stella Bagwell

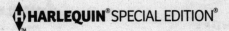

Recycling programs
for this product may
not exist in your area.

ISBN-13: 978-0-373-65098-9

The Cowboy's Christmas Lullaby

Printed in U.S.A.

www.Harlequin.com

After writing more than eighty books for Harlequin, **Stella Bagwell** still finds it exciting to create new stories and bring her characters to life. She loves all things Western and has been married to her own real cowboy for forty-four years. Living on the south Texas coast, she also enjoys being outdoors and helping her husband care for the horses, cats and dog that call their small ranch home. The couple has one son, who teaches high school mathematics and is also an athletic director. Stella loves hearing from readers. They can contact her at stellabagwell@gmail.com.

Books by Stella Bagwell

Harlequin Special Edition

Men of the West

His Badge, Her Baby...Their Family?
Her Rugged Rancher
Christmas on the Silver Horn Ranch
Daddy Wore Spurs
The Lawman's Noelle
Wearing the Rancher's Ring
One Tall, Dusty Cowboy
A Daddy for Dillon
The Baby Truth
The Doctor's Calling
His Texas Baby
Christmas with the Mustang Man
His Medicine Woman
Daddy's Double Duty
His Texas Wildflower
The Deputy's Lost and Found

The Fortunes of Texas: All Fortune's Children

Fortune's Perfect Valentine

Visit the Author Profile page at Harlequin.com for more titles.

To all the nurses who've dedicated their lives
to caring for others.
Thank you.

Chapter One

"Mom, somebody has come to our rescue!"

"Ain't so, Harry! It's a Halloween goblin come to steal our candy!"

Ignoring the shouts of her two sons sitting in the back-seat of the car, Marcella Grayson glanced up from the black dashboard to the flash of headlights in the rear-view mirror.

When her car had suddenly died, she'd attempted to steer it to the side of the rural graveled road. Instead, the vehicle had rolled to a complete stop before she could manage to make that happen. Now the rear end of the car was partially blocking the path of the driver behind her.

Marcella pulled on a lightweight jacket and reached for the door latch. "Stay buckled up, boys. Do not get out of the car for any reason. Understand?"

Harry, the older of the two brothers by a mere eight months, questioned, "Where are you going, Mom?"

"We're blocking the road," she said. "I need to explain to the driver behind us."

"Tell 'em to call the police!" Peter exclaimed. "We need help!"

"Dummy! We don't need the police," Harry chided his brother. "We need a tow truck!"

Marcella didn't waste time telling the boys to quit arguing. Instead, she exited the car and immediately found herself blinded by the orb of a flashlight.

Shielding her eyes with a hand, she peered toward the end of the vehicle, but all she could discern in the darkness was a pair of long, muscular legs encased in dusty denim and an equally dirty pair of cowboy boots.

"Having trouble?"

As the boots started toward her, she tried to recognize the male voice, but failed. She was acquainted with several men who lived or worked here on the Silver Horn Ranch. Unfortunately, this wasn't one of them.

"My car suddenly lost power and quit. Now it refuses to start. And I'm afraid I've blocked the road."

He lowered the circle of light and Marcella's gaze traveled up the long legs, across a wide, deep chest, then finally to a set of chiseled features shaded by the low brim of a black cowboy hat. Tall and thirtyish, he was the epitome of a strong, weathered rancher.

"Don't worry about the road," he said. "If any more vehicles need to pass, I think there's enough room to go around yours."

Relieved for that much, at least, she quickly introduced herself. "I'm Marcella Grayson. My boys and I just left the Calhouns' Halloween party."

He jerked off a scarred leather glove and extended his hand to her. "Denver Yates," he replied. "I work for the Calhouns."

His hand was as hard as a piece of iron and as rough as grit, yet it was warm and reassuring. And for that reason alone, she allowed her fingers to linger against his for a few seconds longer than necessary.

"Nice to meet you, Denver. Thank you for stopping. Of all things, my cell phone has lost its power or something has gone haywire. It refuses to work. So I was beginning to think we were going to have to walk back to the ranch house for help."

He said, "It's at least five miles back to the ranch house. Much too far and cold for you and your children to be walking. I'll take a look at your car. It might be a loose wire or something simple to fix."

"If it's not too much trouble, that would be great!"

"No trouble," he assured her. "Just pop the hood."

Inside the car, she released the hood latch, while Harry and Peter peppered her with questions.

"Is he a bad man? He might rob us!" Peter exclaimed.

"No. He isn't a bad man," Marcella patiently explained. "He's a man who works here on the ranch."

"Does he know how to fix cars?" Harry wanted to know.

"Let's all hope he does," Marcella said while stifling a sigh. She'd already worked a long shift at the hospital today. Her shoulders and legs were aching, and she still had a pile of laundry to do before she could crawl into bed tonight. The only reason she'd agreed to bring her two sons to the Calhoun party this evening was because she'd wanted them to enjoy a real outdoor shindig with a giant campfire, roasting wieners and marshmallows and listening to Orin tell ghost stories. She hadn't expected to get stranded in the middle of the ranch's wilderness.

"Okay. Try to start the motor," Denver called to her from where he stood near the front of the car.

Marcella turned the key, but all that happened was a faint clicking noise.

"It ain't doin' nothin'," Peter muttered with disappointment.

"The guy ain't no mechanic, that's for sure," Harry added.

"All right, you two, I don't want to hear the word *ain't* again. From either of you. In fact, I want complete silence or both of you are going to be in trouble!"

She was tossing them a look of stern warning when Denver Yates pecked on the driver's window.

Marcella lowered the glass a few inches. "Did you find the problem?" she asked hopefully.

"Yes. The battery is dead."

She twisted the key back to the lock position. "Dead!" She groaned with disbelief. "I don't understand. The battery hasn't given me an ounce of trouble! And the car started fine a few minutes ago when we left the ranch house."

He nodded as though to say he didn't doubt her word. "That's the way of batteries nowadays, ma'am. They don't give you any warning as to when they're going to quit. We keep a few batteries on hand back at the ranch yard, but I'm fairly certain none would fit your car. They're mostly for trucks and equipment. Is there someone I can call for you? Maybe your husband can bring a new battery out to you?"

Even if she was still married to Gordon, the man would be about as useful as a rowboat with one oar, she thought drily.

"I don't have a husband," she said flatly. "And I wouldn't ask a friend to drive all the way out here."

If her statement surprised him, he didn't show it. But then, single mothers were the norm these days, rather than the exception.

After a moment, he said, "Sounds like I need to call roadside service for you. But that would be expensive to have them come all the way out here. I could drive you in to Carson City to buy a new battery."

His last suggestion penetrated her spinning thoughts. "No! It's a thirty-mile trip to town, then thirty back. I wouldn't think of asking you to do that. My insurance will pay for the roadside service. I was just thinking—" She glanced back at Harry and Peter, then climbed from the car and shut the door behind her. "Sorry," she said, "but I didn't want the boys to hear me. You see, Peter, my younger son, has asthma. The condition is well controlled, but I don't like him being out in the cold night air for too long. Back at the party he was near the warm campfire. Out here, without the car heater—well, he'll probably be all right until the mechanic arrives, but I'd feel better if you'd drive us back to the ranch."

The man studied her for a brief moment, then glanced at the car's back window. "You don't want the little guy to think he needs special care?"

Surprised that he understood, she decided he must have children of his own. "That's it, exactly. He's ten and wants to think he's just as strong as his eleven-year-old brother."

A faint grin tilted the cowboy's lips. "Sure he does. I won't mention the asthma. So get your sons and whatever else you need from the vehicle and I'll take you back to my place. You can wait there until the mechanic gets your car going."

His unexpected offer caused her jaw to drop. "Your place? I wouldn't want to barge in on you. Lilly and Ava—"

"Are busy wrapping up the party," he finished her sentence. "And I live just a short distance from here."

Deciding she was in no position to turn down help from this Good Samaritan, she said, "Thank you, Mr.

Yates. I really appreciate your help. Uh—but first—well, I hope you won't take offense, but would you mind if I used your phone to call Lilly? Just so she can confirm who you are?"

"Sure. I'm glad you're being cautious."

He pulled a smartphone from a leather carrier on his belt and handed it to her. Marcella quickly tapped out her friend's number and to her immense relief Lilly answered immediately.

After giving Lilly a brief explanation of what was going on with the car and Denver, Lilly assured Marcella she was in safe, capable hands.

When the brief conversation ended, she handed the phone back to the ranch hand. "Lilly tells me you're a nice, capable guy. So if you'll give me a minute, I'll get the boys and my things from the car."

"Fine," he told her. "While you do that, I'll call the roadside service."

Short minutes later, Denver steered his truckload of passengers onto the long drive leading up to his house. Next to him, in the passenger seat, Marcella Grayson's hands were clenched tightly together on her lap as she stared straight ahead at the dark landscape beyond the windshield.

Beneath the dim lighting of the dashboard, he could see enough to tell him the long hair hanging nearly to her waist was a light shade of red, but the thick lashes framing her eyes made it impossible to detect their color. Her features were dainty and soft, and from what he could see, she had that creamy pale skin that only true redheads possessed.

What kind of idiot could have left this little beauty and two boys behind? he wondered. Or had she left him?

What the hell does it matter, Denver? This pretty red-head is none of your business. You need to concentrate on helping her get her car going and forget about all the rest. That's what you need to do.

"Mister, do you know how to ride a horse?"

Denver glanced over his shoulder to see the question had been spoken by the boy called Peter. Tall and thin, with a headful of corn-yellow hair, he had a wide mouth and an eagerness in his voice that said he was basically a curious child.

"A little," Denver said, then realizing the woman was giving him an odd look, he gave her a reassuring wink.

Harry was quick to correct his brother. "Dummy! He's a cowboy and that's what cowboys do. They ride horses!"

"How do you know he's a cowboy?" Peter demanded.

Harry let out a loud sigh of exasperation. "Can't you see his hat?"

"Yeah, but he might be wearing that for Halloween," Peter reasoned.

The exchange between the two boys had Denver smiling to himself. Clearly this was a pair of town kids. Unlike the children who'd been raised here on the Silver Horn and were accustomed to being around ranch hands and livestock.

"Harry, quit calling your brother a dummy," his mother chided. "Peter is asking questions because he wants to learn."

Marcella's statement must have given the older boy the idea to ask his own questions, because the next thing Denver knew Harry had scooted to the edge of his seat.

"I'll bet you have a horse of your own, don't you?" he asked.

"I have five horses," Denver replied.

Clearly impressed, Harry exclaimed, "Five! What do you do with that many?"

Stifling a chuckle, Denver said, "I use the horses to work with. We cowboys have to ride the range, you know. And riding just one horse every day would make him too tired."

"See, numskull," Peter tossed at his brother. "You don't know everything!"

Just as the boys began to argue between themselves again, Denver braked the truck to a stop beneath a low-roofed carport connected to the east side of a wide, rambling house that appeared to be gray in color.

"Here we are," he said to the woman. "Let me turn on the lights and we'll go in."

He climbed from the truck, and after flipping a light on beneath the patio, he opened a side entry door and switched on a light in the mudroom.

Back at the truck, he opened the passenger door and offered his hand up to Marcella. When her fingers clasped around his, he couldn't help thinking how soft and fragile her hand felt against his. And when she stood down on the ground next to him, he noticed she smelled like a mix of wildflowers and campfire smoke, a scent that was oddly appealing.

"Thank you," she murmured. "This is very kind of you, Mr. Yates."

Resisting the urge to clear his throat, he forced himself to release his hold on her hand. "Just call me Denver, ma'am. I'm not used to answering to Mister."

Smiling, she said, "Okay, Denver it is."

He stepped away from her and opened the back door of the truck. "Okay, boys, we're here," he announced. "Unbuckle and climb out."

Once the two children had departed the truck and

sidled up to their mother, he locked the vehicle, then ushered the trio toward the nearest entry to the house.

"I apologize for taking you through the mudroom," he told Marcella, "but the light on the front porch isn't working right now. I wouldn't want any of you tripping over something in the dark."

"Don't apologize," she told him. "We're just happy to be out of the cold. Right, boys?"

"That's right. Thank you, Mr. Yates," Harry spoke up.

"Yeah, thanks, Mr. Cowboy," Peter added.

Inside the kitchen, he flipped on the overhead light to see his unexpected guests gazing curiously around the cluttered room.

Just when Denver was thinking how polite the boys were, Peter spoke up, "Gee, this is messy. Don't you like to wash dishes?"

"Peter!" Marcella gasped, then turned a red face to Denver. "I apologize for my son. He—uh—we don't get out that much. I mean, visit folks in their homes."

Denver chuckled. "Don't apologize. The boy is simply stating the obvious. The kitchen is worse than messy. It's a busy time right now on the ranch. I don't have a chance to do much housework."

"Don't you have a wife?"

This question came from the elder boy, and as Denver looked at him, he didn't miss how much the child resembled his mother, right down to his carrot-topped hair.

Marcella groaned. "I hope you can bear this until the mechanic gets here with the battery," she said to Denver.

"Forget it. I'm used to kids," he told her, then to Harry, he said, "No. I don't have a wife. Or a maid."

"What about kids?" Peter asked.

Even though Denver had been asked that very question many times before, for some reason, having it come from Marcella's towheaded son cut straight through him. "No. None of those, either."

"Sit down at the table, boys," Marcella told the two youngsters. "And be quiet. Mr. Yates doesn't want to be peppered with questions."

"They don't have to sit at the kitchen table," he told her. "They're welcome to sit in the living room. I'll turn on the television and they can watch it while you wait for the car to be repaired."

Mother and kids followed him out of the kitchen and into a long living room furnished with a burgundy leather couch and love seat, and an oversize recliner. In one corner, a television sat atop a wooden console, while a stack of DVDs shared a lower shelf with a remote control.

Marcella took a seat at the end of the couch and instructed the boys to join her. While they settled themselves, Denver turned on the television, then passed the remote to her.

"You'd better choose the channel," he told her. "You'll know what's suitable for them to watch."

Accepting the remote, she gave him a grateful smile. "Thanks. And please don't let us interrupt whatever you need to do. We can entertain ourselves."

"You're not interrupting." Not much, he thought wryly. Having a single mother with a pair of kids in his house was disturbing more than his privacy; it was rattling his normally calm nerves. "So if you'll excuse me, I'll go wash up and see about getting us something to drink. Do you like coffee? What about the boys? Is it okay for them to have soda?"

Harry looked to his mother. "Yeah! Please, Mom."

"Oh boy! Soda! Can we, Mom?" Peter pleaded.

Marcella thoughtfully studied the both of them, then with a resigned shake of her head said, "They've already had so much sugar tonight I guess a bit more won't hurt. I'll help you."

Before Denver could tell her to stay put, she rose to her feet and, after punching a number on the remote, ordered the boys not to move from the couch.

As she followed Denver back to the kitchen, he said, "There really isn't any need for you to help. I'd be making coffee even if you weren't here."

"I'd like to join you anyway. With me out of the room, the boys will hopefully settle down and get engrossed in the program. They're not usually so wound up, but the party was exciting for them," she explained.

Inside the kitchen, Denver went straight to the double sink and began to scrub his hands. His jeans and denim shirt were coated with dust and splotches of dried blood, and manure stained the legs of his jeans. Normally he went straight to the shower when he arrived home from work, but he could hardly take that luxury with Marcella and her children here.

"So do you come out to the ranch very often?" he asked as she came to stand a few steps on down the cabinet counter.

"Not as much as I'd like to. I love visiting Lilly and Ava, but with my shifts at the hospital I don't have many chances to make the drive out here."

"So you work at the hospital?"

"Tahoe General. I'm an RN. I was working third floor for a while, but I'm back in the ER now."

"I see. So you're a nurse like Lilly and Ava."

"Yes. From time to time the three of us worked together. But since they've gotten married and started having children of their own, those days are pretty much gone."

He dried his hands on a paper towel, and though he

would've liked to simply stand there looking at her, he forced himself to open the cabinets and pull out the coffee makings. During the long years he'd worked for the Calhouns, he'd met many of their friends. But not this one. He would've definitely remembered Marcella Grayson.

"You been a nurse for a long time?" he asked.

"Twelve years."

So she'd become a nurse about the same time he'd come to work here on the Silver Horn, he thought. At that time he'd been twenty-four and desperate to start his life over. Since then, she'd acquired two sons. And he'd lost—well, he'd lost too much.

Glancing over at her, he said, "You don't look old enough to have been a nurse for that long."

A wide smile spread her lips, and Denver's gaze was drawn to her straight white teeth and the faint dimples in her cheeks. When she smiled, there was an impish tilt to her lips and crinkle to the corner of her eyes that pulled at him and urged him to smile back at her.

Imagine that. Denver Yates smiling at a woman. A Halloween witch must have put some sort of spell on him tonight, he thought drily.

"That's kind of you to say. But I'm thirty-three. I got my nursing degree before Harry was born. And he's eleven now."

Had she been married at that time? he wondered. A few minutes ago on the road, she'd told him she didn't have a husband, and he'd simply assumed she was divorced. But there was always the possibility that she'd had the children out of wedlock. That wasn't unusual nowadays. Still, Marcella Grayson didn't seem the sort. Not that he knew that much about women. For the past twelve years he'd pretty much avoided having any kind of relationship with a woman.

Annoyed that his thoughts had meandered off on a path he had no business taking, he forced himself to focus on scooping coffee grounds into the filter.

"You must like it—uh, working as a nurse, I mean."

"It's exhausting and the hours are crazy. Especially trying to work them around the boys' needs. But I manage. Most of all, it's rewarding."

He shoved the basket of grounds into place, then stepped in front of the sink to fill the glass carafe with water. By now, she'd moved closer and Denver could only think how odd it seemed to have a woman in his kitchen. How unusual it felt to be looking at her and feeling warm pleasure slowly stirring in the pit of his stomach.

Clearing his throat, he said, "From what Rafe tells me, you nurses are kind of like us cowboys. You have a job that gets in your blood. That's why Lilly still works two days a week."

"That's true. We can't stay away from it. Not completely. At the time I adopted Peter I thought it would be better to quit the hospital and get a job with strictly daytime hours. So I did. I worked in a family clinic downtown for an excellent physician. But after a while I missed the hustle and bustle of the hospital. Especially the ER. So I went back to Tahoe General. That's the good part about being a nurse. You never have to beg for a job."

Denver realized he must be staring at her like some goofy idiot, but he couldn't seem to help himself. Or stop the next question from forming on his tongue. "Your younger son is adopted?"

She nodded. "About three years ago. Actually, Jett Sundell handled all the legal issues for me. With you working here on the ranch, I'm sure you're acquainted with him."

"Sure. Jett's been the Calhoun family lawyer for as

long as I've been here on the ranch." He thrust the carafe under the tap and filled it with cold water. "Plus he's married to Orin's daughter."

"Sounds like you've worked on the Silver Horn for a long time," she said.

"Twelve years." He got the coffeemaker going, then crossed to the refrigerator and pulled out two cans of cola.

She said, "What does your job entail? I know you told the boys you rode the range. But I understand there's much more to running a ranch than that."

He carried the sodas over to the cabinet counter. "I'm manager of the cow/calf operation. I make sure the mama cows are healthy and bred each year by the most productive bulls. That their babies are born safely and grow at the right rate, weaned with as little stress on them as possible, then sorted and sold at the most profitable time. That's just a few of my responsibilities."

She let out a soft laugh, and the sound punched Denver right in the gut. Along with being sweet, it was sassy enough to turn his thoughts to a hot night and sweaty sheets.

"A few? No wonder you don't have time to clean the kitchen!"

What in hell is wrong with you, Denver? You haven't shared sweaty sheets with a woman in years! You haven't even wanted a woman in years! So what are you doing allowing this one to put such erotic notions in your head?

Slapping away the voice in his head, he gestured to the sodas. "Are these okay for the boys?"

"Fine. I'll take them." She walked over to where he stood and picked up the chilled cans. "But I can't promise you won't end up with cola on your floor or furniture. If I made them come in here to the table, it might save your living room."

She was close enough for him to pick up the scent of mesquite smoke and wildflowers in her hair. And as his gaze took in the long red waves dangling against her back, he was struck with the urge to touch the silky strands and feel them slide against his fingers.

"Uh—no need for that," he told her. "There's nothing in the living room the kids can hurt."

She looked at him, and as he met her clear blue gaze, he felt the last bit of oxygen leave his lungs.

"Thanks. I'll be right back." She took the soda cans and left the kitchen.

Denver sucked in a long breath and wiped a hand over his face. What in the hell was coming over him? She was just a woman with two kids and a dead battery. There was nothing about her, or the situation, to turn him into a randy teenager. Besides, in an hour or so, she'd be gone and he'd never see her again.

Between now and then, he was going to have to get a grip on his senses and remember he was a widower. It wasn't meant for him to have a woman or a family. Not now. Not ever.

Chapter Two

When Marcella reappeared in the kitchen, Denver had already filled two mugs with coffee and placed them, along with a sugar bowl and container of powdered creamer, on the table.

"The boys are watching a sci-fi movie," she said cheerfully. "Between space monsters and Orin's ghost stories, they'll probably wake up with nightmares."

"Well, that's what Halloween is all about—getting spooked by imaginary creatures." He gestured toward the mugs. "The coffee is ready. I'll let you fix your own."

"Mmm. It smells heavenly." She stepped over to the table and began to spoon creamer and sugar into the steaming liquid. "This is very nice of you. And I'm feeling very awful about intruding into your home. Believe me, if Peter hadn't been with me, I wouldn't have minded waiting in the cold."

She stepped away from the table and Denver moved close enough to collect his mug.

"You say he has asthma. Is that something he developed recently?"

She shook her head, then after a careful sip of coffee said, "No. He's had the condition since he was very small.

About two years old from what I can gather. I first met Peter when he was admitted to the hospital with asthma. He was—"

Her words broke off and Denver suddenly spotted a shimmer of tears in her eyes. She was a woman who felt deeply about others, he realized. Maybe that was the nurse in her, or simply her maternal feelings showing, but no matter the reason, it touched him in a way that he hadn't expected.

"Sorry," she said huskily, then forced a smile to her face. "I get emotional when I think back to the first time I saw Peter lying there struggling to breathe. He was... so frail and sick. You see, Peter's biological parents had abandoned him. A very old grandfather was trying to care for him, but he was too poor and decrepit to take care of himself, much less a child. But that's all in the past, thank God. He's mine now."

Denver didn't know what to say. He was too busy trying to imagine this dainty little woman opening her heart and her home to a lost child. Not just for a day or two. Or even a week or a month. She'd welcomed him into her family for a lifetime. He wasn't even sure his late wife could've shown that much compassion and devotion.

Swallowing away the tightness in his throat, he said, "Peter's a lucky little boy."

She laughed lightly. "He doesn't think he's all that lucky whenever I have him and Harry washing dishes or pushing the vacuum cleaner."

Relieved that she was lightening the moment, he gestured to the dirty dishes stacked in the sink. "It's pretty obvious that guys don't much care for cleaning chores."

She chuckled, then an idea appeared to suddenly strike her. "I'd be happy to do the dishes for you," she offered. "It's the least I can do for all your help."

She was already making the place feel too homey, Denver thought. He didn't want to imagine how he'd feel to see her standing at the kitchen sink washing his dirty dishes. As though she belonged there.

"Thanks. But I'll take care of this mess later. Let's take our coffee out to the living room," he suggested.

Moments later, Marcella joined the boys on the couch and Denver took a seat in a big armchair that was angled to her left. At this time of the evening, she suspected he normally stretched out in the recliner across the room, but he must have decided that making himself that comfortable in front of his guests would show bad manners.

The idea made Marcella feel even more like an intruder, but then, he'd given her little choice in the matter. Damn, damn, if her battery was going to die, why couldn't it have done it back at the big ranch house? At least there she would have felt comfortable and welcome.

The rueful thought brought her up short and she mentally shamed herself. She and the boys were complete strangers to Denver Yates, yet he'd opened his home to them. She needed to be thinking grateful thoughts toward the man instead of wishing she was anywhere else but here.

It wasn't his fault that his big, masculine presence was making her feel hot and bothered. Or that looking at his rugged face was sending very unladylike images through her head. And why would she be thinking about kissing a man, anyway? Men were nothing but trouble, and for the past ten years she'd made it just fine without one.

Sipping her coffee, she glanced at Harry and Peter. Both her sons' attention was glued to the television screen. Since the music was building to a frantic crescendo and the last monster was about to meet his doom, the movie was clearly reaching the end.

She glanced over to Denver and was jolted by the fact that he was looking at her.

"Uh—do you watch much television?" She realized the question probably sounded inane to him, but this whole situation had knocked her off-kilter. No doubt tomorrow she'd look back on it and groan with embarrassment.

He said, "Not much. News. Weather. The farm and ranch report. Things like that." His lips twisted to a wry slant. "I'm not big on entertainment. Guess my job gives me more than enough to think about."

She smiled. "I'm sure you've heard the old adage about all work and no play."

"Yeah. It makes a dull boy," he said with a faint grin. "Sorry. I guess I am pretty boring."

She clutched her coffee cup even tighter as she tried to keep from laughing. He was the furthest thing from boring that she could imagine. In fact, she couldn't remember the last time she'd encountered a man who'd interested her as much as this big rancher.

"I wouldn't say that. You're not boring me." Oh my, she sounded like a teenager instead of a thirty-three-year-old mother, she thought. Clearing her throat, she added, "I'm sure you and Rafe have plenty of exciting stories to tell. Were you with him and Bowie when the stallion got loose and ran off into the mountains?"

Surprise arched one of his brows. "You know about that?"

She nodded. "Lilly and Ava told me all about it. Rafe was black-and-blue from the spill he took when his horse fell."

"I was helping with the hunt," he said. "But I wasn't riding in the area where Rafe fell. We were fortunate that only Rafe got hurt that night. The weather turned really nasty with snow and ice."

"I don't understand you ranchers. You're always wanting lots of snow to put moisture and nitrates into the ground, but doesn't that make terrible conditions for the cattle?"

"If the snow gets too deep it causes problems. Or if we have blizzard conditions. The worst case is when calves are being born in that sort of weather. We try to see that all of them make it. Unfortunately, we lose a few. Those are the times when the ranch hands might get an hour or two of sleep each night."

She shook her head. "I don't think I could bear seeing a baby animal of any kind struggle."

He looked straight at her, and Marcella found her gaze traveling over his chiseled features. Once they'd come into the house, he'd removed the black cowboy hat from his head. Now as the dim glow of a shaded lamp cast an orb of light over him, she noticed the thick wave falling over his forehead was the color of dark chocolate. The kind that was supposed to be good for your health, she thought wryly. She figured Denver would be just as tasty as a piece of dark chocolate. But good for her health? No, in her opinion, he looked like a massive heartache.

"I'm sure you see people struggling in the ER," he said. "Animals are no different. They need help, and we cowboys do our best to give it to them. Just like you nurses do for people."

"I wasn't thinking of it in that way. But you're right. Except that we nurses get to work under the best conditions," she reasoned. "You ranchers are dealing with the raw elements."

She felt a tug on her arm and glanced around to see Harry holding up the television remote. "The movie is over, Mom, and the stuff showing now is no good. Would you change the channel?"

"Excuse me," she said to Denver, then turned her attention to finding some sort of program to hold the boys' attention. After a moment, she parked the channel on a child-appropriate sitcom. "There. That's the best I can do."

"Aw, Mom, that's goofy stuff for girls," Peter complained.

"Yeah," Harry seconded his brother. "We want to see cops and car chases."

"Yeah," Peter chimed in. "Or spaceships and laser fights."

"Sorry, boys. Take it or leave it," Marcella said firmly.

A pout came over Peter's face and he looked to Denver for support. "I'll bet when you were a kid you got to watch good stuff. Not boring stuff like giggling girls."

Marcella watched Denver glance her way, before he turned his attention to Peter.

"Actually, I never watched much TV," he said.

"You didn't?" Harry asked, clearly mystified by the rancher's statement. "What did you do? Play computer games?"

Denver chuckled and Marcella was struck by the sound. It was rich and warm and so pleasant she wished she could hear it again.

"No," he answered Harry. "Back when I was your age, we didn't have a computer at home. Or smartphones. Sometimes, when I went to town, I'd play video games with my friends."

"You didn't live in town?" Peter asked. "Where did you live? Here?"

He shook his head, and though Marcella knew she should scold the boys for asking personal questions, she was just as curious as they were about their unexpected rescuer.

"No. I lived on a ranch in Wyoming with my parents. I mostly stayed busy helping my dad with ranching chores. When I wasn't doing that, I was riding horses or doing my homework."

"Homework. Ugh!" Peter complained. "Nobody but bookworms likes that stuff."

"Nobody wants to be dumb," Denver reasoned. "And you need to do your homework to get smarter."

"Me and Harry don't have a dad," Harry said with a shrug. "We just have Mom. She plays baseball with us. But she doesn't know all that much about boy things. Like fishing. Do you know how to fish—for trout?"

"I've done a little fishing. Not much."

Peter scooted to the edge of the couch. "I don't want to learn how to fish. I want to learn how to ride a horse and run really fast! As fast as the wind!"

Harry looked at his brother and rolled his eyes as though he was eons older rather than a mere eight months. "You're just saying that because of Mr. Yates. Yesterday you said you wanted to be a doctor."

Peter's head tilted from side to side in contemplation. "I still do. I wanta make people well, like Mom does. But I can do that and ride a horse, too. Can't I, Denver?"

He exchanged a knowing glance with Marcella before he answered Peter's question. "Sure. Doctors can ride horses, too. So can people who fish for trout."

Harry thought about that for a moment, then said, "Yeah, I guess it would be fun to run fast. As long as I didn't fall off."

Marcella said, "You have to learn how to walk the horse before you run it. I'm sure Mr. Yates didn't run the first pony he got on."

Denver chuckled again and the sound came as a relief to Marcella. Maybe she and the boys weren't getting on his nerves too badly. The idea had her studying him from beneath her lashes and wondering things she shouldn't be wondering. Like why he wasn't married. And why he had no children of his own. A man like him would have no trouble finding a woman who'd be more than willing to give him a family.

Maybe he'd already tried marriage and had gotten a divorce, Marcella silently contemplated. Or could be some woman had soured him on love and put him off the idea of marriage. Or perhaps he simply wanted to keep his freedom. Whatever the reason for his bachelorhood, Denver's personal life was none of her business.

"I was a baby when my dad put me on a pony," Denver spoke up. "So I don't remember the occasion. But I can assure you there wasn't any galloping done that day."

"Orin told us ghost stories," Harry said. "One was about Little Joe the wrangler who was trampled in a stampede. He said his ghost rides the hills and the desert flats. Have you ever seen him?"

"A few times," Denver said, then tossed her a sly smile.

Marcella felt as enthralled by this man as her sons seemed to be, which should have made her feel foolish, but it didn't. Tonight was a party night for fun, and it had been a long, long time since she'd spent a few enjoyable moments in a man's company.

"Really?" she asked impishly.

"Cross my heart," he said with feigned seriousness. "He wears a black-oiled duster and rides a white horse."

Peter jumped to his feet with excitement. "That's right! And the horse's mane and tail looks like flames! When did you see him? At night?"

"Usually at night. But once, some of the ranch hands

and I saw him in the late afternoon riding through a patch of Joshua trees. A big storm had blown up and turned the sky dark. Lightning was flashing everywhere and jumping like streaks of blue fire off the horns of the cattle. The herd stampeded and we raced our horses after them."

"What happened?"

The question came from both boys, and as Marcella studied their mesmerized faces, she couldn't help but dream and wish that she could give them the father they needed and deserved. Her mother was constantly harping for her to date, to make an effort to find a man willing to marry her and be a father to her sons. But Marcella didn't want a marriage of convenience. She wanted love. For herself and her boys. They deserved nothing less.

Denver said, "The cattle were running straight toward a deep gorge and going so fast we couldn't catch up. They were all going to fall over the cliff and die. Then suddenly out of nowhere Little Joe appeared from the black, boiling clouds. His white horse was so fast it was a blur in the wind and they turned the herd just in time."

"Wow! That must've been cool!" Peter exclaimed.

"What happened then?" Harry asked. "Did you see Little Joe up close?"

Denver shook his head. "By the time we reached the gorge, he was gone. But we thought we heard the sound of his horse's hooves echoing down in the canyon. It gave us all the shivers."

"That's awesome!" Harry spoke in a breathless rush, then turned an excited look on his mother. "Mom, did you hear that? Mr. Yates saw a ghost! A real ghost!"

"Well, I'm sure Mr. Yates has seen a lot of…strange things out on the range," she reasoned.

"Tell us some more, Mr. Yates," Harry pleaded. "Orin

told us about a headless prospector and he walks around with a pickax. Have you seen him?"

"Boys, that's enough for now. Mr. Yates has had a long day. And—"

Before she could finish, Denver's cell phone rang. Marcella and the boys went quiet while he answered the call.

Once he tapped the face of his phone to end the conversation, he looked over at Marcella. "The mechanic is finished with your car. So if you and the boys are ready, I'll drive you back to it."

When the car had gone kaput, she'd been thinking of the endless chores she needed to get done at home and lamenting the time that was going to be wasted waiting on a mechanic to repair it. Now all she could think was that she wasn't quite ready to leave Denver's company.

"Oh, Mom, do we have to go right now?" Harry asked.

Peter quickly seconded his brother's suggestion. "Yeah, Mom, do we? We want to talk to Mr. Yates some more."

Forcing herself to her feet, she motioned for the two boys to join her. "Sorry, fellas. It's getting late and we've already interrupted Mr. Yates's evening enough. Come on. Pull on your jackets and gather up your empty soda cans."

Less than ten minutes later, the boys were loaded in the backseat of the car. She'd filled out the necessary forms for the repair cost, and the mechanic had driven away.

Now as she stood outside the driver's door with Denver less than two steps away, she'd never felt so awkward or deflated in her life. An hour ago, she was desperate to get home. Now she was reluctant for her time with this man to end. It made no sense. None at all.

"There's no way I can begin to explain how much I

appreciate your help," she told him. "And thank you for being so patient with Harry and Peter. I imagine tomorrow your ears will still be ringing."

With a wry smile, he shook his head. "Not at all. I enjoyed their company. It made me remember back to when I was that age."

She said, "You might not believe this, but they don't normally have such motormouths. Especially with a person they've just met. They like you."

"I'm honored."

She hadn't expected him to say anything close to that. But then everything about him and this evening had caught her off guard.

"Well, I'd better be going."

She extended her hand to him, but instead of shaking it, he wrapped both hands around hers. The contact felt incredibly intimate, and for a moment she wondered if she'd forgotten how to breathe.

"Goodbye, Marcella. It was nice meeting you and your sons. Have a safe trip home."

It was nice meeting her, she thought, but not nice enough to ask for her phone number, or mention he might like seeing her again. The notion filled her with disappointment, but she wasn't about to let it show. Instead, she gave him the cheeriest smile she could muster.

"Thanks, Denver. And you be careful to watch out for Little Joe," she teased. "You know Halloween is actually tomorrow night. He and that white horse might be on the prowl."

He grinned. "Right. I'll keep my eye out."

"Goodbye," she said, then slipping her hand from his, she quickly turned and climbed into the car.

Once she'd shut the door and fastened her seat belt, she didn't allow herself to glance at him through the window. Instead, she drove away and tried her best not to notice the lights of his truck reflecting in her rear-view mirror.

Chapter Three

A week later, Marcella was nearing the close of her Friday shift in the ER when fellow nurse and friend Paige Winters walked up behind her.

"Dr. Sherman is being his usual nasty self again," she said with a weary sigh. "Thank goodness our shift is nearly over. He can take out the rest of his sour attitude on the next crew of nurses instead of us—or me, I should say. The man has had the evil eye on me ever since I came to work in the ER. I'd give anything to slap that smirk of his right off his face."

"Including your job?" Marcella asked as she yanked a soiled sheet from an empty bed.

"Well, no. I love my job here at Tahoe General too much to let one moody doctor ruin it."

Marcella tossed the dirty sheet into a nearby hamper, then turned to see that the other nurse had already started fitting a clean sheet on the just-stripped mattress.

Paige was a year or two younger than Marcella, and though she was a natural redhead, like her, Paige's shoulder-length hair was a deep wine color that contrasted vividly with her pale gray eyes. She was an extremely hardworking, dedicated nurse, and Marcella had often hoped that the other woman would find a man to love her. She deserved that much from life and more.

From the opposite side of the narrow bed, Marcella said in a hushed voice, "Dr. Sherman isn't giving you the evil eye. He's giving you the eye. Period."

A fiery blush spread across Paige's cheeks. "I am so tired of everyone hinting that Dr. Sherman has the hots for me," she muttered. "The man is as cold as an ice cube. He wouldn't know what to do with a woman if she fell right into his arms!"

"Nurse Winters! I need you down here! Pronto!"

The sound of Dr. Sherman's bellow from the opposite side of the treatment room put a tight grimace on Paige's face.

"See? He's a jerk in a lab coat. And not nearly as good-looking as Dr. Whitehorse, who's been giving *you* the eye for months now."

The other woman hurried away, making it impossible for Marcella to deflect Paige's remark about Dr. Whitehorse. Sure, the man was young and handsome and nice. She liked him as a friend, but he just didn't make her heart go pitter-patter. Not the way that darned cowboy up on the Silver Horn had done.

Denver Yates. This past week she'd thought of little else. And the fact that Harry and Peter kept bringing up his name didn't help matters at all. From the remarks they made, she could tell both of them expected to see Denver again. Preferably in the near future. And she hadn't had the heart to burst their bubble. Neither of them would understand that enduring friendships rarely grew out of chance meetings.

You need to forget the cowboy, Marcella. He probably has a girlfriend. And even if he doesn't, he'd hardly be interested in a mother with two kids. Wake up! A hunky man like Denver can have his pick of women. You can bet he's already put you and your sons in the very back of his mind.

Doing her best to shove the miserable voice out of her head, she finished the last few minutes of her shift, exchanging patient information with the fresh group of nurses. By the time she'd changed clothes and headed out to the parking lot to her car, seven o'clock had turned into seven forty-five.

She was climbing into her car when she heard the cell phone inside her purse ringing. The caller was most likely her mother, she thought wearily, wondering why she hadn't yet been by to pick up the boys. After twelve years of Marcella working long, erratic shifts as a nurse, her mother still didn't understand her schedule would never be predictable.

After starting the car, she pulled out the phone and was surprised to see it had been Lilly Calhoun ringing, rather than her mother. Since her friend never called just to chat, Marcella decided to take a minute to return the call. If something had happened on the ranch, she wanted to know about it.

"Hi, Marcella," Lilly answered cheerfully. "Sorry to bother you at this hour. Are you home from work yet?"

"No. I'm still in the parking lot. Is anything wrong?"

"No. Everything is great. I'll just keep you a minute. I wanted to ask if you're free tomorrow night. I'd like for you to come to a little dinner party I'm having."

Marcella frowned. "Dinner party? Lilly, I was just out to the ranch last week at your Halloween party."

"So? That was mainly for the kids. This is just for us adults."

So that meant she'd have to tell Harry and Peter she was going to the Silver Horn without them. That would definitely cause a fuss. But on the other hand, Marcella was entitled to an evening out on her own once in a while.

"Is this some sort of special event? Someone's birthday?" Marcella asked.

"Nothing special. There will only be a few of us. The men are getting together to talk business and Ava and I don't want to be bored to death. You can at least entertain us with hospital news."

"I am off tomorrow," Marcella said thoughtfully. "And it would be nice to have some adult conversation. I'm not sure what Mom will say about watching the boys. If she's planning on a bingo night, forget it."

"Don't worry. If Saundra can't watch the boys, then bring them with you. Tessa will be keeping all the kids upstairs in the playroom. She won't mind watching Harry and Peter, too."

Rafe and Lilly had a young daughter and son, while Ava and Bowie's baby boy was only a few months old. Tessa would have her hands full without adding Harry and Peter to the mix.

"I'm not sure—"

"I won't let you refuse," Lilly interrupted. "This is important."

Marcella countered, "Lilly, you just said this wasn't anything special. Are you—"

"I only meant it was important to me that you come," she quickly explained.

Marcella absently massaged her forehead while watching a group of nurses exit the back of the building. She let out a weary sigh. "Okay, I'm too tired to argue. I'll be there. What time?"

"Great! Make it about six thirty so we'll have plenty of time to enjoy a cocktail before dinner. And in case you need more persuasion, Greta is cooking prime rib," she added. "And coconut cream cake."

Marcella chuckled. "Pure blackmail. I'll see you tomorrow night. Right now I have to get home. Uh, who's doing all that crying in the background?"

"Austin. He's crying for me to take him over to the barn to see his daddy."

"Then you'd better pull on your boots and take him and big sister, Colleen, to the barn."

Lilly let out a good-natured groan. "Sure. Give the little man everything he wants. If Austin grows up to be a spoiled brat, I'm going to tell everyone Nurse Grayson ruined him."

Laughing, Marcella told her friend goodbye, then ended the call.

The next evening, Denver quit work at an early hour, and after checking in with Doc Simmons about a pair of sick cows, he headed home to shower and change for the dinner party at the big ranch house.

Managing the cow/calf operation made it necessary from time to time for him to attend business meetings with the Calhouns. Especially with Orin, the father of the five Calhoun brothers, and Clancy, the eldest son and general manager of the Silver Horn. There were also occasions when issues cropped up with local ranchers and Denver needed to make an appearance at a town gathering. But parties were a different matter, and for the most part, he avoided them as much as possible. Yet for some mysterious reason, tonight Rafe had been adamant that he attend Lilly's small dinner party.

Rafe had said he and Orin wanted to use the evening to discuss some new feed ideas. Denver didn't believe a word of it. In the twelve years he'd been working on the Silver Horn, the feed program had remained consistently the same. The whole idea had him wondering if Lilly was giving someone a surprise party and Rafe was wanting to keep the celebration a secret. Whatever reason, Denver would have preferred to stay home and catch up on a bit of rest.

Frowning at his image in the bathroom mirror, he smeared a handful of shaving cream over his jaw and chin. Who was he trying to kid? He'd gotten home early for the past several nights. At least, seven o'clock was early for him. But he hadn't rested or enjoyed the solitude. He'd spent most of the time cleaning the kitchen and thinking about Marcella Grayson and her two sons. And damn it all, he was still thinking about them.

You're a fool, Denver. The world is full of pretty nurses and single mothers. It's also full of gamin-faced boys with a penchant for asking questions. There is nothing special about the little family.

Maybe not, Denver argued with the nasty voice in his head, but there'd been something very special about the way they'd affected him. Being near Marcella, holding her hand, even for those brief moments, had reminded him what it was like to hold a woman in his arms and make love to her. And the boys—well, they'd made him remember all that he'd lost back in Wyoming.

When Marcella arrived, Tessa, the Calhouns' young housekeeper, nanny and maid all rolled into one, met her at the door.

"Good evening, Marcella," she greeted warmly. "It's so nice to see you again so soon. Let me take your coat and bag. Everyone is out back on the patio having drinks."

Marcella shrugged out of her coat and handed it and her clutch bag to the slender young woman with light brown hair and a gentle face. "Outside? Maybe I should keep my coat. It's rather cold to be having drinks outside."

"Orin has built a fire in the fire pit, so I imagine it feels nice and cozy." She glanced at Marcella. "Wow! You look so pretty tonight. That emerald green dress looks gorgeous with your red hair."

Feeling more than self-conscious, Marcella glanced down at the simple sheath dress she was wearing. Since her wardrobe was limited to mostly work or casual clothes, she didn't own much in the way of party wear.

"Lilly didn't say whether this was going to be a fancy dinner. But knowing her, I decided I should at least wear a dress."

Tessa laughed as she went to hang Marcella's coat in a nearby closet. "You know Lilly and Ava, they like to find any reason to dress up. Come along," she invited, "and I'll walk with you back to the patio."

Even though Marcella wasn't a frequent visitor to the ranch, she'd been there often enough to know her way around the massive three-story house. Yet each time she walked through the opulent rooms, it amazed her that two of her best friends had married into such a wealthy family.

As soon as the two women reached the family room and the sliding glass doors that opened onto the patio, Tessa quickly excused herself.

"I'll leave you to join the others," she said. "The kiddos are upstairs with their great-grandfather Bart. He's watching them until I can take over. Uh—I thought you might be bringing Harry and Peter with you tonight. Didn't they want to come, too?"

If there'd been a chance of them seeing Denver again, the boys would've jumped at the chance to make the trip out here. Otherwise, they'd been content enough to spend the night with their grandmother. "My mother is making them a special treat for dinner tonight."

"Well, maybe next time," she said.

The housekeeper hurried away and Marcella let herself through the glass door and onto a large rock patio partially covered by a low hanging roof. As she carefully fastened the door behind her, she heard Lilly's voice calling to her.

"Marcella! You're finally here!"

Turning, she found the willowy blonde standing right behind her, and Marcella quickly gave her friend a tight hug.

"Finally here," Marcella repeated with a light laugh. "You say that like I'm the party honoree or something."

"Well, you are important to us around here," she said with an impish smile, then after another quick hug, she curled her arm around Marcella's waist and urged her across the patio. "Come on and have a seat. It'll be a while before Greta serves dinner. Want something to drink? Orin has made a pitcher of margaritas if you'd like one."

"No. I'll be driving home later. I'll just have a ginger ale."

"I'll get it," Lilly said. "You go on over and say hello. I'm pretty sure you know everyone here tonight."

Marcella started toward the group of people gathered around the huge brick fire pit. Ava and Bowie were standing with their backs to the warm flames, while Clancy and his wife, Olivia, were snuggled together on a cushioned wicker love seat. Nearby Rafe, his dad, Orin, and Colley Holbrook, the manager of the horse division, were talking with a man seated with his back to Marcella.

The moment Ava spotted her approach, the tall brunette hurried over to greet her with a swift kiss on the cheek.

"Come over by the fire," she invited with a happy smile. "Gosh, you're looking lovely tonight. Where did you get those heels? They're very sexy."

Marcella chuckled. "They're hand-me-downs from Mom. She bought them, then decided they were too risqué for her."

"Lucky you."

"Here's your ginger ale," Lilly announced as she joined the two women. She handed Marcella the glass of ginger ale. "Let's go find a seat where it's warm."

As the women approached, the men all politely rose to their feet to greet Marcella.

"I think you know everyone here tonight," Lilly said, then added teasingly, "Although it's been so long since Clancy and Olivia have shown their faces around here, you might not recognize them. Once they built their house up on the mountain, we can hardly get them down here for dinner."

Marcella shook hands with the ranch manager and his pretty wife, who worked in the land management division for the BLM.

"Yes, it has been a while," she said as she shook hands with each of them. "Nice to see you again. How's your little boy, Shane?"

"More like his grandpa Orin every day," Clancy teased. "Growing into a real rascal."

While Orin chuckled loudly, Olivia added, "He's nearly three years old now and we can't turn our backs on him, or he'll be in the barn trying to climb on the back of a horse."

"He and Austin are two peas in a pod," Lilly spoke up jokingly. "When those two cousins get a little older, we're going to have hell to pay."

Ava put her hand on Marcella's shoulder and turned

her slightly to the left. "You have met Denver, haven't you? He's a lot like Clancy—you have to twist his arm to get him here for dinner."

Denver! The man who'd been occupying her thoughts for the past week was standing right in front of her. The surprise of seeing him very nearly caused her jaw to drop, but she caught herself before that could happen and forced a cheery smile on her face.

"Uh—yes. We have met," she said.

He extended his hand to her. "Hello, Marcella. It's nice to see you again."

Lilly had said this was going to be a simple gathering. What was he doing here?

Hoping she didn't appear as caught off guard as she felt, Marcella placed her hand in Denver's. And just like the last time, something in the bottom of her stomach flipped over. Then over again.

"Hello, Denver. How are you?"

A faint smile touched his lips, and as Marcella's gaze zeroed in on his face, everything around her suddenly faded, except him and the feel of his big rough hand wrapped around hers.

"Fine. Thanks for asking."

The feel of his gaze slowly meandering over her face was causing heat to pool in her cheeks. And just as she was telling herself it was time to extricate her hand from his and put an end to the strange buzzing in her head, she heard Lilly speak behind her.

"There's Greta at the door. Let's go in, everyone. Dinner is served."

Denver dropped her hand and they both began to gravitate toward the back of the house with the rest of the group.

"Sounds like it's time to enjoy Greta's cooking," he said. "I hope you brought your appetite."

She'd been as hungry as a horse until she'd turned and saw him. Now her nerves were so scattered she could scarcely think about eating.

Stop it, Marcella! You're not a teenager with a sudden crush on the cool rebel in senior class. You're a thirty-three-year-old mother. Far too old to be getting the vapors over a sexy man.

She said, "I haven't eaten anything since early this morning. So I'm ready to eat."

"Did Peter and Harry come with you this evening?"

"No. They're with their grandmother tonight. I didn't want to overload Tessa with kids. They'll be disappointed they missed seeing you."

"I'm disappointed they're not here," he said.

His simple statement sounded so sincere, yet she told herself not to take it to heart. There were plenty of guys who pretended they liked kids. Until they were asked if they wanted to be a father, and then they stumbled backward, as if they'd just faced a rattlesnake.

With everyone in the house, the group quickly migrated to a dining room that was beautifully furnished with a carved oak table and chairs, along with a matching sideboard and massive china cabinet. Down the middle of the vast table, vases of orange and gold marigolds mixed with burgundy-colored mums alternated with flickering fat brown candles. Across the room, a row of arched windows revealed a starry night sky competing with the glow of lights illuminating a portion of the ranch yard.

The beauty of the Silver Horn never failed to impress Marcella, but tonight she wasn't absorbing her surroundings as much as usual. Instead, every cell in her brain was focused on the tall, muscular rancher standing a few steps away.

"Ava and I didn't bother assigning seats. So everyone just grab a chair," Lilly announced. "Except for the end seat. That's for Granddad Bart, of course."

"You're wasting your breath, Lilly girl," Bart boomed out as he took his seat at the head of the table. "Everyone already knows this is my seat. When I'm dead and gone, my son gets it. After that, you grandsons can fight over it."

Dressed in a crisp white shirt and dark slacks with his thick gray hair brushed neatly back from his rugged features, at eighty-eight, Bart looked as though he was still fit enough to wrestle a bear and ornery enough to try it.

Orin pulled out a chair to his father's right. "Dad, we're not going to discuss your passing tonight or any night for that matter. These beautiful women don't want to hear such morbid talk."

"Son, I'm eighty-eight years old. What the hell do you think is going to happen? That I'm going to live forever?"

"You're mean enough to live forever, Granddad," Bowie spoke up teasingly. "So I say you better not mess around and get nice on us. We might lose you."

"Bowie! That's awful," Ava scolded her young husband.

With a wry shake of his head, Orin looked down the table. "Denver, would you help Marcella into her seat? I'm sure you won't mind sitting next to our pretty guest tonight."

"My pleasure," Denver said.

He stepped over to the table and pulled out the chair nearest to Marcella. As she sank into the padded seat, she felt as though everyone in the room was watching the two of them. And suddenly she wondered if this whole evening had been a setup to throw her and Denver together.

But that was crazy thinking. She hadn't voiced any interest to Lilly or Ava about the cowboy. Had Denver mentioned something about her to some of the Calhouns? She couldn't imagine that. He didn't seem the type to discuss private issues. Even with his friends.

Glancing up at him, she smiled faintly and murmured her thanks. "Sorry. Looks like you're stuck with me for a dining companion tonight."

"I'm sure I'll manage to survive," he said in a voice only she could hear.

Near the head of the table, Orin said, "Sorry, Colley. You just happened to be on the wrong side of the table tonight."

"It's okay, sir," the horse trainer said. "I don't think I'll be getting lonely anytime soon."

Marcella glanced over at the young man who'd taken a chair next to Bowie. From what Lilly told her a couple months ago, Colley's wife had divorced him and left town with a man she'd worked with at a financial firm in Carson City. No doubt he was still seeing red whenever he looked at a female.

While the remainder of the group took their seats at the table, Denver had made himself comfortable in the chair next to Marcella, and she found it impossible to keep her attention away from him.

"Lilly told me this was going to be a small group tonight," she said to him. "I was surprised to see you here— I mean, I've never seen you here for dinner before."

He shrugged, and Marcella's gaze was drawn to his broad shoulders and the faint movement of muscle beneath the finely woven fabric of his dark gray shirt. A leather bolo tie fashioned with a silver accent set with coral stones was pushed tight against his throat, while matching cuff links fastened the cuffs at his wrist. He looked dark and dangerous and oh so handsome.

"That's because I don't visit the big house that often. Rafe twisted my arm to get me here tonight."

Marcella's mind began to spin. No way would Lilly and Ava go to this much trouble to throw her and Denver together at the same dinner table. Or would they? For the Calhouns, this gathering was little more than a regular family dinner.

"Oh. Well, Lilly twisted mine. So looks like we're in the same boat tonight."

"I'm here to discuss a new feed program with Orin and Rafe. So far that hasn't happened," he said. "Why were you invited?"

"To catch Lilly and Ava up on hospital news. So far that hasn't happened, either," she added with an impish smile. "But no matter. Getting to eat Greta's cooking is worth the drive out here."

"As long as your battery doesn't die again," he added jokingly.

She felt her cheeks turning pink. If only he knew how much she'd been thinking of him since that night he'd welcomed her into his home. He'd probably want to have Colley trade chairs with him, she thought.

"I'm happy to say I haven't had any more car trouble," she told him.

Before he could make any sort of reply, Bowie caught Denver's attention, and then Greta appeared with a loaded trolley and began to serve the first course. Marcella glanced down the table to Lilly, and the cunning little smile on her friend's face left no doubts as to what this dinner party was all about.

The only thing that could save her from this embarrassing situation now, Marcella thought, was if Denver never discovered how the two of them had been pushed at each other.

Chapter Four

As usual, the food was mouthwatering, but Denver could have been eating hay and not noticed the difference. Having Marcella, looking like a dream and smelling like a meadow of wildflowers, sitting next to him throughout the long dinner had jangled his senses.

When she'd first appeared on the patio earlier this evening, he'd been shocked. Although on second thought, he shouldn't have been all that surprised. She was good friends with Lilly and Ava. For all he knew, she might be a regular dinner guest.

However, during the past week, he'd been telling himself he'd never see the beautiful nurse again. Then she'd suddenly been standing in front of him. It was like his daydreams had suddenly come to life.

A few minutes ago he'd watched Marcella leave the room and so far she hadn't returned. Damn it, why was he noticing her comings and goings, anyway? She was just a pretty friend of the Calhouns and certainly nothing to him.

"Denver, would you like more cake?"

He glanced up to see that Lilly had paused in front of the chair where he was sitting in the family room.

Smiling, he shook his head. "Thanks, Lilly. It was delicious, but I couldn't hold another bite."

She gestured toward the opposite end of the room, where a long bar stretched across one corner. At the moment Bowie was playing bartender to Clancy and Rafe. The brothers were joking and laughing and obviously enjoying the evening. Denver was glad to see the men so relaxed. To an outsider, it probably appeared that the Calhouns had an easy life. But Denver knew firsthand how tirelessly Orin and his sons worked to keep the ranch thriving.

"Bowie has been spiking his brothers' coffee with apricot brandy," Lilly said with an impish grin. "You might want to join them."

His senses were already whirling enough, Denver thought. He didn't need to make them worse. "Thanks, but I think I'll stretch my legs a bit and walk out by the fire."

"Great idea," she said, then added, "If the fire needs more wood, there's plenty stacked on the end of the patio."

Denver thanked her, then left the chair and slipped through the glass doors and onto the dark patio.

The night air had turned very chilly, but the fire was still burning, warming the area around the fire pit to a comfortable temperature. Grabbing a chair from the shadows, he started to drag it closer to the fire when he heard a female voice off to his left.

"You must have needed some fresh air."

He glanced around to see Marcella walking out of the shadows. Where had she come from, he wondered—another part of the house?

"I thought I'd come out and enjoy the fire." He gestured to the chair. "Have a seat. I'll drag up another."

She smiled and thanked him, and while she made herself comfortable, Denver went after another chair. By the time he'd rejoined her in the orange glow of the firelight, he was wondering if he was the luckiest man alive or the most ill-fated. Sitting out here in the dark with a beautiful redhead could be detrimental to his health, mainly his ability to think.

As he took a seat a short distance away from her, she said, "I've been upstairs visiting the kids. So I thought I'd come out here and enjoy the fire a bit before I rejoined everybody in the family room."

"Do you have a fireplace in your home?" he asked.

She grunted with amusement. "Even if I did, I couldn't afford to buy wood to burn." She looked over at him. "I noticed you had a fireplace in your living room. Do you use it very often?"

"No. Although there's plenty of dead wood up in the mountains here on the Horn that I could gather and burn. By the time I get home in the evenings, it's easier just to let the heating system do its job." Maybe if he had someone to sit with him and share the warmth of the flames, he'd feel differently, Denver thought. Maybe someone with soft curves, long red hair and lush pink lips that tilted at the corners would make building a fire all worthwhile.

"My grandparents live in Northern California in the countryside out from Redding," she told him. "When my brother and I were just youngsters, Grandfather would build a campfire for us. We thought it was wonderful."

He looked over at her and inwardly groaned at the sight of her delicate features bathed in firelight. Just more pleasant memories he'd have to try to erase from his mind, he thought.

"You have a brother?" he asked.

"Yes. He's four years younger. He was married for a while, but now he's divorced."

"You see him often?"

"When he lived in Carson City, I saw him regularly. But he moved back to Redding to be near our grandparents. Which is a good thing. Since they're getting older, they need help around the farm." She cast him a curious glance. "What about you? Do you have siblings?"

"A sister. She's five years younger than me. She lives in Gillette. Our parents live near Moorcroft. That's a little town not far away."

"Do your parents still ranch there?"

The fact that she remembered that much about him not only surprised Denver, but it touched him in a way he never expected. Sure, he could find a woman to have a drink with, or even share a bed with. But none of those women cared about the things that were important to him. This one did seem to care, and that made her very different.

It also makes her as dangerous as hell, Denver. Marcella is a family woman. She's not looking for casual sex. If she ever went to bed with a man, it would be out of love. Not to ease a basic urge. Just keep remembering that when you look into those sky blue eyes of hers.

He cleared his throat while trying to rid himself of the voice of warning going off in his head. "Yes. Thankfully Dad is still in good health and able to handle the daily work. Mom helps, too. She's pretty good with horses and a rope."

Marcella smiled at him. "Sounds like you came by ranching naturally."

"It's the only life I've known," he admitted. "What about you? Was your mother a nurse?"

She laughed softly. "Not hardly. Mom panics at the

sight of blood. My grandmothers weren't nurses, either. It was just something that called to me when I was about twelve years old. I like helping people—helping to make them feel well and whole again."

All the nurses and doctors in the world hadn't been able to help Christa. But Denver didn't want to think about her or that part of his past. He'd spent the past twelve years trying his best to forget it. Now was hardly the time to let those dismal memories start creeping in. Or maybe it was the perfect time, he argued with himself. Maybe tonight, more than ever, he needed to remember why he couldn't let himself get interested in a woman like Marcella. And yet just sitting here with her by the fire made him feel like a ton of weight had been lifted from his heart.

"Does your mother work?" he asked. "I mean, an outside job."

"Yes. She's a waitress in a downtown restaurant. Believe it or not, she used to have a nice office job as a secretary to a banker. But it was too stressful. She likes being out among people."

"And your father?"

"He works for a real estate firm over in Sacramento. He never cared for farming like his father up in Redding."

"So your parents aren't together anymore?"

She shook her head. "No. They divorced when Spence and I were teenagers. They're still friendly, though. And neither one of them ever remarried. I think they still love each other, but throw them together for more than two hours and an argument will break out. You're very lucky, you know, that your parents are still together and work together. I think that's so nice."

Lucky. Yes, in so many ways Denver knew he was blessed. But there were plenty of times, like tonight, when he looked at the Calhoun brothers with their devoted wives and growing families, that he felt like a man with a missing limb. He was surviving without any problems. But a part of him longed to feel whole again.

"Yes. My parents are special," he replied.

She rose from the chair and backed up to the fire. Denver tried not to notice how the firelight silhouetted her curvy shape or the way it turned her auburn hair into a fiery glow around her head.

"You must like your job here on the Silver Horn a lot," she said.

"Guess it's obvious."

She smiled faintly. "You've been here a long time. Twelve years, didn't you say?"

"That's right. When I first came here, I wasn't sure I would like it. I'd never worked on a ranch this big before. But the Calhouns are special people. They made it feel like home. And made it clear that I was appreciated. That means a lot."

Her expression sober, she nodded. "I guess you must have been here when Claudia, Orin's wife, died."

In spite of the fire, Denver suddenly felt cold inside. He'd been working here on the ranch for only two years when Claudia had taken that tragic fall down the staircase and fatally injured her head. Seeing Orin lose his wife so soon after Denver had lost Christa had been like being hit by an avalanche. He'd had to dig himself out of the misery all over again.

"Yes," he said stiffly. "It was tragic for him. For the whole family."

"I'm glad he's dating Noreen now," she commented. "But frankly, I'm surprised he hasn't married her yet."

"I'm not," he said bluntly.

Her brows arched slightly, and Denver knew his remark had surprised her.

"Oh. You say that as if you know what's holding him back."

"I do. You see, I'm a widower, too."

She stared at him as everything from shock to empathy flickered across her face. "I'm sorry. I had no idea."

He shrugged. "Don't be sorry. You didn't say anything wrong. Besides...it happened a long time ago."

She let out a heavy breath. "Well, I feel awful anyway. If I'd known, I wouldn't have mentioned anything about Claudia and Orin."

"Forget it," he said quietly, then added, "Please."

She hugged her arms to her and Denver realized she must be getting cold.

He said, "If you're getting chilly, I can build up the fire."

"No. I should probably be going back in. I told Ava and Lilly I'd visit the kids for just a few minutes. If I don't show up soon, they'll be going upstairs after me."

He didn't want her to go. He wanted to sit here with her for hours. Just the two of them alone. He wanted to keep hearing her voice and smelling her flowery scent. He wanted to touch her and feel her touching him.

Had he suddenly lost his mind? Or was he just now waking up after a long sleep? Either way, she was shaking him in ways that were downright scary.

Rising to his feet, he stood next to her and stared into the flames licking around the chunks of mesquite and pine.

"Yeah, I guess I should go back inside, too," he admitted. "Orin and Clancy still haven't brought up the subject of the feed program. I think they've forgotten the reason I'm here for this gathering tonight."

She cleared her throat. "I don't think they've forgotten."

Intrigued by her comment, he turned his head and allowed his gaze to slide over her profile. "What do you mean?"

After a brief hesitation, she said, "I'm not sure. Actually, what I'm thinking is…almost too embarrassing to repeat. But I'm beginning to think I should."

He stepped in front of her. "What are you thinking?"

"It's a good thing we're standing in the dark," she mumbled. "Or you'd see that my face is actually the same color as the fire."

"I don't get it."

The sound that came out of her was supposed to be a laugh. Instead, it was more like something was stuck in her throat. "No. You wouldn't. Because—well, I think Lilly and Rafe must be playing Cupid."

His jaw dropped. "You mean—you and me? They think we—" He didn't know how to finish. Like her, he was embarrassed. But not for the same reasons as Marcella. Long before Rafe had invited him to dinner he'd actually been thinking of her in those terms.

"Yes. That's exactly what I'm thinking."

He blew out a long breath. Now that he thought about it, Marcella's presumptions all made perfect sense. And he didn't know whether to be annoyed with his friends or grateful.

Without warning, she reached over and rested her hand on his forearm. The gentle touch was all it took to decide how he felt about being pushed in her direction.

"I apologize, Denver. I haven't said anything about you to Lilly. Other than the fact that you called roadside service for me."

He shook his head. "That's the only thing I told Rafe. How your car broke down and I helped you."

She pulled her hand away from his arm and let out a short, awkward laugh. "At least we got a prime rib dinner out of the deal."

The loss of her touch made him want to gravitate closer to the warmth of her body. "Well, the way I see it, since Lilly and Rafe have gone to so much trouble, I'd hate to disappoint them. Wouldn't you?"

Confusion puckered her forehead. "I don't understand."

The grin he put on his face belied the anxious rhythm of his heart. "We might as well make them happy and go out on a date together. What do you say?"

Her mouth formed a shocked O, and Denver had to fight not to bend his head and kiss the look of surprise off her lips.

"A date? With you?"

Chuckling, he glanced around at the shadowy patio. "I don't see anyone else around here but me."

Her gaze lifted to his and Denver suddenly wondered if the aftershock of one of California's tremors had rippled across the border. Something was sure tilting him off-kilter.

"I have to be honest, Denver, I haven't dated in a long, long time. I'm not sure I even remember how."

"I haven't dated in a long time, either. And I'm not sure I *ever* knew how," he told her.

She laughed then, and the sound caused Denver's spirits to soar. Mistake or not, his heart had never felt this light or carefree in years. And it wasn't wrong to want to enjoy the feeling while it lasted. Even if it was just for tonight.

"Okay," she said. "I accept."

"Good. So what kind of date would you like? Dinner and a movie? Dancing? Live theater? Sports?"

She shot him a suspecting look from beneath her

lashes. "For a man who hasn't dated in years, you sure rattled off that list pretty quickly."

He gave her a lopsided grin. "The single ranch hands talk about their lady friends. Left to my own imagination, I'm boring."

Her expression said she wasn't buying that, and he chuckled again.

"I'm serious, Marcella. A man who spends his days astraddle a horse and his attention zeroed in on herds of cows and calves couldn't be anything but boring to a woman."

Shaking her head, she smiled. "Well, I'll make it easy for you. Why don't I cook dinner for you at my place? Peter and Harry will be thrilled to see you again. Uh— unless you're worried about eating my cooking."

An evening in her home with her two sons. It would hardly be the romantic situation he had in mind. But for now, he wasn't about to pass up the chance to spend more time with this woman.

"I'm not worried at all," he assured her. "Just tell me when and where."

Her expression suddenly softened, and then before he knew what was about to happen, she rested a hand against the middle of his chest and rose up on her tiptoes. When she placed a lingering kiss on his cheek, he very nearly groaned out loud.

"What was that for?" he asked, his finger massaging the spot on his face where her lips had tasted.

"That was a small thank-you," she said softly. "For being such a good sport about all of this. Most people don't like being manipulated."

"In this case, I'm a willing participant."

Before she could make a reply to that, Denver bent his head and captured her lips with his. She tasted sweet and mysterious, and though he was trying hard to keep the kiss to a slow, simple search of lips, he couldn't stop his hands from slipping to her back and drawing her closer.

When he finally eased back enough to look down at her, he could see that her eyes were closed and her nostrils flared like a skittish filly with bolting on her mind.

Licking her lips, she turned her head aside and drew in a deep breath. "I suppose you can explain what that was for."

"That was for Lilly and Rafe…just in case they might be looking. It'll give them something to think about."

A week later Marcella was still thinking about the kiss Denver had planted on her lips when they'd been alone on the patio. He'd said it was for Lilly and Rafe's sake, but they'd both known that was a ridiculous fib.

Once they'd gone back inside the house, Lilly had gone to the kitchen and Rafe had been sitting on the same stool at the bar. Neither had been anywhere close enough to witness the kiss. Thank God, Marcella thought. She didn't want anyone, even her closest friends, knowing she'd kissed the Silver Horn's ramrod like he was something special to her.

"What are you looking for, Marcella? Maybe I can help you find it?"

Marcella glanced away from the medical cabinet to see Paige had walked up behind her.

Sighing, Marcella answered, "I'm looking for a pair of deep brown eyes fringed with thick black lashes."

A comical look of confusion came over Paige's face. "What? Are you having a stroke?"

Marcella let out a short, humorless laugh. "What makes you think that? My speech isn't slurred."

"It's not your diction that has me concerned! It's what you're saying! Brown eyes? Hmm. Chet Anderson has gray eyes, I think. And I believe Dr. Whitehorse's eyes are sort of a greenish-hazel color. What guy around here has brown eyes?"

Chet Anderson, the director of nursing, was a nice guy. So was Dr. Whitehorse. But looking at either one of them didn't make her feel all gooey inside. The way she felt whenever she laid eyes on Denver. God help her.

Turning back to the cabinet, Marcella pushed several small boxes of gauze and prewrapped bandages to one side of the shelf. "He's not here in the hospital. And I'm—well, you should be worried, Paige. Because I think I've turned into a complete idiot."

"A man? You've lost your mind over a man?" Paige asked incredulously. "When did this happen? Tell me! Tell me!"

Finding the container of swabs she'd been searching for, Marcella closed the cabinet and faced the inquisitive nurse.

"Two weeks ago. He's the ramrod over the cattle division on the Silver Horn Ranch."

"Why are you just now telling me about this?" Paige asked, clearly annoyed that Marcella had kept this important news to herself.

Marcella wrinkled her nose. "Because I wasn't going to mention it to you. Period. It's just a…momentary, one-sided thing. Nothing will come of it. I know it and he knows it. But still, I can't seem to stop thinking about him. Silly, isn't it? I never thought I'd ever meet a man who'd make me gaga in the head."

Suddenly all smiles, Paige glanced around the dispensary to make sure no one was in earshot. "So when do you plan to see him again?"

Rolling her eyes, Marcella started out of the small room with Paige trotting right behind her.

"Tomorrow night. I'm cooking dinner for him."

"Wow!" Paige exclaimed. "A family-type date already? You're working fast, my dear!"

Marcella groaned. "You don't understand. It's for safety reasons. I need the boys as chaperones."

Paige's mouth fell open. "Oh! You mean the cowboy is that much of a wolf? I need to get a look at this guy!"

"Not him, silly!" she muttered under her breath. "It's me I'm worried about."

Paige laughed out loud. "You? A she-wolf? That's a good one."

"About as good as that one standing over there," Marcella said, as from the corner of her eye she spotted Dr. Sherman staring at the two nurses. "I think Dr. Do-Good is motioning for you."

Paige glanced across the treatment room, which, for once in a blue moon, just happened to be empty of patients at the moment. As soon as she eyed the doctor crooking his finger at her, she muttered through tight lips, "I'd like to tell him exactly what he can do with that finger."

"Why don't you? It might be good for him to see he's not the only one around here with a temper."

"Yeah. Sure, Marcella," she said drolly. "I'd like to keep my job."

"You can always transfer upstairs. Maybe pediatrics? Internal?"

"Those are sounding better every day," she said, then hurried off to see what the doctor was demanding next.

Trying to push the ever-lingering thoughts of Denver

from her mind, Marcella carried the swabs over to one of
the curtained units and refilled the empty jar on the small
work counter. Behind her, she could hear the commotion
of a patient being wheeled in by the EMS.

Thankful for the distraction, she hurried out of the
space to assist with the emergency.

On Sunday evening, Denver drove slowly through the
residential street, searching for the house number Marcella had given him the night of the Calhoun party. He'd
never been in this area of Carson City before, so it all
looked new to him. But then Denver wasn't one to visit a
person in their home, he thought wryly. Especially when
that person was a woman.

Since losing Christa, he'd never wanted to get that
chummy with a female. And he wasn't exactly sure
why he'd agreed to this type of date with Marcella. The
woman wasn't his sort. She was the kind who wanted
and needed a husband. A role he never planned to take
on again. Not in this lifetime. But he'd been so charmed
by Marcella, he hadn't been able to refuse her. And after
that kiss they'd shared by the fire, she could've asked
him to go to Mars with her and he would've jumped on
board the rocket ship.

*Get this through your head, Denver. This will be your
first and last date with Marcella. After tonight you're
going to say goodbye and leave it at that. For your sake
and for hers.*

Marcella's house came into view, and as he parked his
truck behind her little economy car, he tried to pocket
away the words of wisdom going off in his head. Tomorrow he could worry about putting an end to this unexpected interest in Marcella. But for tonight he wasn't

going to think about that. For the next few hours he was going to pretend he was no different from any other man who wanted a wife and family.

Chapter Five

Moments later, at the door of the white-and-green bungalow, the sight of Marcella's cheery smile warmed Denver like a ray of spring sunshine.

"Hello, Denver. Please come in."

She pushed the door wide, and he stepped past her and into a tiny foyer.

"Did you have any problems finding the place?" she asked as she fastened the door behind them.

He glanced around to see she was dressed casually in a pair of snug-fitting blue jeans and a yellow sweater that made her red hair appear even more vivid. The clothing clung to her curves, and he couldn't stop his imagination from trying to picture her with nothing on, except the taste of his kiss.

Clearing his throat, he said, "No. Your directions were good. But for the weekend, I was surprised at how quiet the neighborhood seemed."

"It's Sunday evening," she explained. "Most folks around the neighborhood have gone to evening church services."

He handed her a plastic sack containing two cartons

of ice cream. "For dessert," he explained. "Vanilla and rocky road."

"Oh! How thoughtful. The boys are going to love this. Thank you, Denver."

Removing his gray cowboy hat, he raked a hand through the flattened waves while giving her a smile. "You're welcome. I hope I haven't kept you and the boys from church services. I could've come for dinner on a different night."

She took his hat and motioned for him to follow her out of the foyer. "Don't worry about it. We went to Mass this morning. And anyway, my shifts in the ER are always changing. I never know when my nights will be free."

He followed her into the living room, and while she placed his hat on a wall table, he glanced around the cozy space. Furnished with a long couch, two armchairs and a wooden rocker, it was clearly a room that was used for relaxing. In one corner the television was playing, although the volume was turned low, making it impossible to tell what the caped hero on the screen was saying. In a far corner he spotted a big round basket with two cats curled inside. Since their sleep hadn't been disturbed by his arrival, Denver assumed the felines were accustomed to noise.

As she noticed him surveying the room, she said, "The boys were watching a movie, but I told them to go wash up," she explained. "You're welcome to take a seat in here and catch your breath. I still have things to attend to in the kitchen. Dinner is almost ready."

"I'll go with you to the kitchen. Maybe I can help you finish up," he suggested.

"Great. I'd appreciate a helping hand. If you don't mind. I promise not to ask you to wash any dishes."

The impish smile on her face had him grinning back at her. "I'm not too worried about that," he told her. "I'll be glad to help."

No, Denver thought, as he followed Marcella out of the room, dipping his hands into a sink full of dishwater was the least of his worries. He was more concerned about the sway of her little rounded bottom and the way her long hair tumbled down her back like rippling flames. Everything about her was working on his senses in a wicked way, and he wasn't at all sure he could resist the temptation.

The two of them had barely stepped into the kitchen when he heard footsteps racing through the house, and then a pair of voices were calling loudly.

"Denver!"

"Denver's here!"

Denver turned toward the sound and was immediately tackled by both boys. Laughing, he gathered them close and ruffled the tops of their heads.

"Hello, guys." Their eagerness to see him again was definitely a surprise to Denver. And so was the feeling of having two pairs of little arms hugging his waist with all their might.

Marcella turned away from the freezer, where she was finding a place for the ice cream. "Peter! Harry! Let Denver go before you squeeze the air out of him!"

The boys stepped back but remained close enough to hang on to his arms. Denver looked over their heads and smiled at Marcella. She returned his smile, but he could tell from her expression that she was equally surprised by the boys' enthusiastic greeting.

"Aw, Mom, we're just happy, that's all," Harry told her.

"Yeah," Peter chimed in. "We didn't think we'd ever see you again, Denver."

Denver hadn't thought he'd be seeing Marcella and her boys again, either. Now, because of Rafe and Lilly, he was standing here surrounded by the little family and wondering if he'd gotten himself into far more than he'd ever expected.

"Well, he's here now," Marcella spoke up. "So give him some space. In fact, you boys need to set the table while Denver helps me with the glasses and ice."

Though both children grumbled a protest, they promptly went to work putting plates and silverware around a small rectangular table made of dark wood. Denver ambled over to the cabinet counter a few steps down from where she was pulling a large dish from the oven.

"The glasses are in the cabinet to your left," she told him. "And the ice maker should be full. I made tea to drink. But if you don't care for it, I have other things."

"Tea is fine." He went to work fetching glasses from the cabinet. "Whatever is in that dish sure smells good."

"Lasagna," she told him. "I hope you like it."

From across the room, Harry said, "We told Mom to fix steak. 'Cause that's what cowboys like to eat. Steak and beans. Right, Denver?"

Denver smiled to himself as he filled four blue glasses with crushed iced. "That's what the cook in the bunkhouse says."

"But Mom said we had to have hamburger meat tonight," Peter explained. "'Cause it's cheaper."

Denver couldn't help but laugh out loud.

With an embarrassed groan, Marcella shook her head. "Okay, I've been ratted out, so I might as well confess," she said to Denver. "I did go the cheaper route."

Still chuckling, he said, "Don't worry about it, Marcella. The ranch supplies its employees with beef throughout the year. Believe me, I get more steak than I want."

She glanced at him. "Really?"

"Really. And I love lasagna."

Her gaze caught his and her lips tilted into a grateful smile. "I'm glad."

Denver was glad, too. Glad he'd been brave enough to ask her for a date. To come here tonight and be a part of her family, even if it was for only one evening.

Moments later, the simple meal was ready to eat and everyone was seated around the table. Marcella had insisted he sit at the end, while she'd taken a seat to his right and the boys sat to his left.

As Denver looked over the table, he tried not to feel out of place. Especially since all three of them were looking at him as though he belonged in the head chair. Dear heaven, how would it feel if he was actually sitting at the head of the table, looking out at his wife, his children? No. That was for other men to experience. Like the Calhoun brothers. Not Denver.

"This is fine," he said to Marcella in a joking voice, "But I'm not Bart Calhoun. I don't need a *special* chair."

She laughed lightly. "Bart wants to remind everyone that he's the boss. I don't believe you're quite as authoritative as him."

"He's not as old as Bart, either," Harry added sagely.

Marcella exchanged an amused look with Denver before she folded her hands and glanced across the table. "Peter, would you like to say grace tonight?"

"Sure, Mom."

Peter bowed his head and everyone followed suit.

"Dear Lord," he prayed, "thank you for our food. Even if it is hamburger. Thank you for my mom and my brother. And thank you for letting Denver be with us. Amen."

By the time Denver lifted his head, his throat was too tight to say a word. Thankfully, Marcella did it for him.

"Thank you, Peter. That was very nice," she said. "Now let's everybody dig in. And, guys, I want to see salad in your bowls. More than what a little rabbit might eat, too."

Once everyone had started to eat, Peter looked over at Denver. "Do you know how to cook stuff like Mom does?"

"Well, I can cook, but I doubt I can make things as good as she does."

Harry frowned at his brother. "He has to know how to cook, dummy. He doesn't have a wife, so he has to do it himself."

"He could eat stuff like bologna and potato chips," Peter shot back.

Marcella leveled a stern look at her elder son. "Harry, what have I told you about calling your brother *dummy*? I don't want to hear it again. Otherwise, there'll be no television for you tonight."

"I'm sorry," Harry mumbled sheepishly. "I don't mean he's a real dummy. Peter gets it."

"Yeah," Peter added, "like I call Harry an idiot. He ain't no idiot. I mean, he isn't an idiot. He's actually pretty smart."

Marcella glanced over at Denver, and he could see she was trying her best not to smile. Denver was finding it very difficult to keep from laughing out loud.

After plates were filled and everyone began to eat, Marcella asked, "So what's happening on the ranch now? I imagine at this late date in the year all the calves have been born and the horses have delivered their foals."

"That's right," he replied. "The big thing now with my job is making sure all the calves are weaned and vaccinated before winter sets in. Weaning puts such a stress on the babies it sometimes causes them to develop shipping fever. So we want them strong and well over that before cold weather hits."

"What's shipping fever?" Peter asked as he scooped up a huge bite of noodle.

"That's sort of like when a person gets a really bad cold or the flu," Denver explained in a way the boy might understand. "When animals get shipping fever, they have to have shots to get well. Like humans sometimes do."

"Mom knows how to give shots," Harry said proudly. "She can make people well."

"Yeah," Peter added. "I bet she could make a calf well, too."

"My sons think I'm some sort of super nurse. Except when it comes time for them to take nasty-tasting medicine," she said with a laugh. "Then they think they know more than me."

"I take my medicine like Mom tells me," Peter spoke up. "Now I don't have asthma anymore. That makes me happy."

Harry reached over and rubbed an affectionate hand over his brother's head. "Peter can run all he wants to now and he doesn't get sick. Mom made him all well. She's pretty special."

Denver glanced over to see a blush staining her cheeks. The self-conscious expression made her even more beautiful to Denver. That and the fact that she had to be one of the most giving, loving women he'd ever met.

"Yes, she's pretty special," Denver agreed.

Earlier, before Denver had arrived, Marcella had sat the boys down and given them instructions on how to behave in front of their guest. The main one being not to be jabbering constantly at the dinner table. But their short-term memory had apparently failed. Neither Harry nor Peter had allowed the conversation to lapse for more than ten seconds at a time.

By the time the meal was over and Marcella had shooed the children out of the kitchen, she let out a long sigh.

"If your ears are still ringing tomorrow, come by the ER and I'll have the doctor treat you."

"My ears?" he asked curiously as he helped her clear the dirty dishes from the table. "Have I been saying huh a lot or something?"

She chuckled and was amazed at how comfortable it felt to talk to him about simple things. During the few dates she'd gone on in the past, she'd worried about every word that had come out of her mouth. But with Denver, she didn't feel the need to try to make impressive conversation. Something about him made her feel like being herself was all he wanted.

"No," she said, "I meant ringing from all that chatter at the dinner table. I'm sorry about that. The boys promised me they'd be quiet. Somehow they must've let my instructions slip their minds."

Smiling, he shook his head. "I'm glad they did. I can't remember the last time I've laughed so much. I'd forgotten how much fun it is to be their age. They're good kids, Marcella. You should be very proud. You've done a great job with them."

She'd been given compliments before, but coming from Denver made it feel far more special. "Thanks. I've been blessed."

"They obviously adore you. But do they ever talk about wanting a father?" he asked, then quickly added, "I'm sorry. I shouldn't have asked such a personal question. Just forget it."

She glanced over as he scraped the leftovers on a plate into one of the salad bowls.

"Don't be silly. Your question is perfectly normal. And believe me, it's a fact I wrestle with quite a lot. I try not to feel guilty because they don't have a father. But I do. I understand how much they need a man in their lives to guide them—love them. But I'm not the sort of woman to marry just for their sake. I suppose that seems selfish of me, doesn't it?"

Without glancing her way, he stacked a pair of glasses onto the scraped plate. "No. Why should you enter a marriage of convenience? You deserve more than that. So do the boys."

She let out a breath she hadn't realized she'd been holding until now. "Thanks for saying that. Believe me, my mother is constantly reminding me I need to think more of the boys than myself. She's very good at laying the guilt trip on me."

Smiling faintly, he picked up the dishes and carried them over to the double sink. "I love my mother very much. But I'd never let her tell me what I need to do with my life. Or not to do. The way I see it, once a kid grows up, he needs to make his own mistakes."

She let out a good-natured groan as she joined him at the sink. "I've made my share of those, and Mom doesn't let me forget them, either. And since she works in such a public job, she's always trying to get me to go on dates with some of the regular guys who come into the restaurant."

Leaning a hip against the cabinet counter, he leveled an amused look at her. "So it's not just Lilly who's trying to set you up with dates."

Groaning again, she shook her head. "My mother is the worst. But I guess you can see what I think about her choice of men. I've been divorced for nearly eleven years. And I'm pretty sure that isn't going to change."

"Hmm. Why are you certain you'll remain single? You're young and attractive. I'm sure you've had plenty of offers."

Offers, yes. But not the matrimonial kind, Marcella thought ruefully. "I'm trying to forget the kind of offers I've had since I divorced Gordon," she said, injecting as much humor as she could into her voice. "Most of them were fairly short-term. Like one or two nights."

A stretch of awkward silence passed until he finally said, "That's hard to believe."

"Not really." She carried the leftover salad to the cabinet and dumped the greens into a plastic storage bag. "Taking on two children is a huge responsibility. Emotionally and financially. I understand that. So I'm really not expecting to find a man who'd want all three of us."

"Well, I can see where you have to put your boys first. That's the way it should be."

She looked at him and smiled while hoping he couldn't see the lonely sadness in her heart. When she and Gordon had first gotten married, they'd both been very young and impetuous, but she'd loved him. He'd been a happy, fun-loving guy. Until the responsibilities of growing up and being a husband and father had hit him. Then it had quickly become obvious to Marcella that he hadn't been geared for either task. In the end, divorcing Gordon had been the right thing to do for both of them.

After her broken marriage, she'd vowed she would never get herself emotionally tangled up with another man unless she was very, very sure she could trust her heart to him. Now, after all these years, she'd practically given up on finding that special man.

Clearing her throat, she said, "Let's dish up some of

the ice cream you brought and we'll take it to the living room. I'm sure Harry and Peter are more than ready for dessert. The boys have a DVD they want you to see. Some sort of old Western."

"Sounds good, but what about cleaning the kitchen?"

She smiled at him. "We're going to put that task on hold."

Much later, after the ice cream had been eaten and the cowboy movie watched, Marcella announced it was time for the boys to brush their teeth and go to bed.

"Aw, Mom, it's not late," Harry argued.

Peter backed up his brother. "We don't want to go to bed while Denver is here."

"I'm sorry, guys," she told them. "Tomorrow is a school day. So hop to it."

The two brothers had been lying on a braided rug in front of the television, but their mother's firm order had them both climbing to their feet.

"Can Denver come see our room?" Harry asked. "I want him to see my posters."

Peter added, "Yeah, and I want him to see the picture I drew."

Marcella tossed a questioning glance at Denver. "Do you mind?"

"Not at all."

"Okay," she told the youngsters. "Go get ready for bed and I'll bring him to your room."

Seemingly satisfied with their mother's promise, Peter and Harry scurried out of the room. Marcella rose from where she'd been sitting on the couch and began to gather up the empty ice cream bowls.

"I'll carry these to the kitchen and be right back," she told him.

After she'd left the room, Denver looked around him and wondered what he was really doing in this house with this little family. He wasn't looking for marriage. He didn't want a wife or kids. And that was what Marcella was all about. To expect her to want anything less from a relationship would be insulting.

Before he said goodbye tonight, he had to make it clear that they wouldn't be seeing each other again. Unless it was just a friendly encounter on the ranch.

He was wondering how he could go about telling her without seeming like a jerk when she suddenly reappeared. The smile on her face made him want to groan with misgivings. How could he think about not seeing her lovely face again? Not seeing the warmth of that smile and feeling it radiating to the very depths of him?

"Come on and follow me," she said. "I'm sure the boys have given their teeth about thirty seconds of brushing and jerked on their pajamas."

Rising from the chair, he trailed her out of the living room and down a short hallway to a door on the right. After rapping lightly on the facing, she opened it and gestured for Denver to precede her into the children's room.

Dressed in matching blue pajamas, Peter and Harry practically leaped at him, each boy grabbing Denver by the hand and tugging him deeper into the square space.

"Well, this is really nice," he said as he glanced around the room furnished with twin beds and a large chest of drawers. "I didn't have a brother to share a room with, so I had to stay all by myself. You guys are lucky."

"We like it together," Harry said. "I was really happy when Mom got me a brother."

"And I was happy she got me one, too," Peter added with a toothy grin.

Harry pointed to the bed next to the inner wall. Both

beds were covered with dark brown comforters. At the foot of each one was a pile of dirty clothes and athletic shoes.

"This is where Peter sleeps. And I sleep in this bed by the window. Unless we have a lightning storm, and then I get in the bed with Peter."

That admission brought a giggle from both boys.

"Yeah, we don't like lightning," Peter informed him. "Neither do Gus and Mabel. They hide under the bed."

The walls were covered with colorful posters and school paraphernalia, while built-in shelves held books and toys and sports items. It was a typical boy's room, and seeing it hit Denver in a spot he'd thought was long dead.

"Sorry it smells like a locker room in here," Marcella told him.

Denver chuckled. "We guys aren't supposed to smell like flowers."

"That's right, Mom," Harry agreed. "We're supposed to stink a little."

Hiding a smile, Denver turned his attention to the posters on the wall. Most of them were scenes from popular children's movies, and some were images of major league baseball stars.

Harry tugged him across the room to where more pictures were pinned to a closet door. "Look at this one, Denver. Peter drew this. He says it's you. I told him you probably didn't have a dog, but he drew one on there anyway."

Amazed, Denver took a closer look at the pencil drawing. It was an incredibly lifelike image of a man on a horse riding through the desert. A dog with long hair and a bushy tail was trailing the horse's heels. This was how Peter pictured him, Denver thought. And the little boy had cared enough to put the image on paper. He didn't know what to think.

His throat tight, he said, "Oh my, Peter. You're a regular little artist! This is awesome."

"That's what I told him, too," Harry said as proudly as if he'd done the drawing himself.

Peter reached up and unpinned the piece of heavy-weight paper from the door. "Here," he said to Denver, "you can have it if you want it."

Denver accepted the drawing and tried to ignore the swell of emotions in his chest, but the feeling was like nothing he'd ever experienced before and he was forced to swallow several times before he managed to speak.

"Thank you, Peter. I'm going to be sure to frame it."

Behind him, he felt Marcella moving into the room. "Okay, guys, it's getting late. Hop into bed and say goodnight to Denver."

Not wanting to push their luck, Peter and Harry jumped into their respective beds, and after settling their heads on the pillow, they gave Denver a pair of gamin-like grins.

"Good night, Denver. Come see us again real soon. Will ya?" Harry asked.

"Yeah, will ya?" Peter added.

What are you going to do now, Denver? Tell these boys you don't want to get involved with them or their mother? If you tell them that, you'd be more than a liar. You'd be a coward along with it.

Forcing a smile on his face, he said, "I'll try my best to see you soon."

Marcella moved past him, and after pressing a kiss on each boy's forehead, she turned off the lamp on the nightstand.

Denver told them good-night, then followed Marcella back out to the living room.

When she sank onto one end of the couch, he said, "I guess I should be going. You probably have a long day ahead of you tomorrow, too."

She patted the cushion next to her. "Don't worry about my schedule. Please stay a few more minutes. We really haven't gotten to talk much with the boys monopolizing your attention."

Sitting alone with Marcella in a quiet room was not exactly the best way to protect himself against her charms. But he couldn't resist.

He eased down on the cushion next to her. "All right, if you're sure I'm not overstaying my welcome."

Drawing her legs up beneath her, she squared around slightly so that she was facing him. "Of course not. Besides, I needed this time alone with you to apologize."

Denver allowed his gaze to travel over her heart-shaped face with its upturned nose and clear blue eyes. Her creamy skin was spattered with pale freckles, and her lips were plush and velvety. Just thinking about the way they had tasted was enough to make his gut clench with desire.

"I can't imagine why," he said, his thoughts turning his voice husky.

"You asked me to go on a date and I put you through this. I shouldn't have done this to you. It wasn't right or fair."

He shook his head. "What are you talking about?"

"This wasn't just an evening with me. It was an evening with me and my family. I wouldn't blame you if you never spoke to me again."

"Do you hear me complaining?"

Her gaze dropped sheepishly to her lap. "No. You're too nice for that."

"Nice," he repeated the word gruffly. "You can't imagine the things I've been thinking for the past two hours. Most of them aren't...nice."

Her lips parted and Denver's gaze froze on the plump curve of her lower lip and the edge of white teeth.

"No doubt. You've probably been thinking you'd like to choke me for putting you through this."

"Not choke you, Marcella. I want to kiss you. Like this."

He didn't give her time to leap off the couch or evade his arms as they curled around her shoulders. Instead, he drew her close and covered her lips with his.

Chapter Six

Denver's plan had been to make the kiss a short exploration. He'd never intended for it to get out of control. But the moment their lips made contact, something exploded and desire took control. Before he realized what he was doing, his hands were at the back of her head, his fingers meshing into her silky hair. His tongue was thrusting between her teeth, daring hers to join his in an erotic dance.

While their mouths fused tighter and tighter, her arms slipped around his neck and the front of her body pressed against his. She felt like a warm, beautiful dream. One that he never wanted to let go.

The kiss went on and on, robbing his breath and drugging his senses. This was what his life was missing. This hot, sweet connection was the craving that gnawed at him on a nightly basis, and he didn't want to lose it. He wanted it to go on and on.

Somewhere in the midst of his thoughts, he heard her groan, and then the two of them were falling sideways in a tangled embrace. But before Denver could shift them to a more comfortable position, she was pushing her palms against his chest in a clear plea for him to give her space.

Reluctantly, he eased his lips away from hers and she instantly scrambled to a sitting position. As he watched her wipe the tangled hair from her face, hot desire simmered in his loins. Yet at the same time he felt a great need to protect her feelings.

"I'm sorry, Marcella. I didn't mean for that to happen. I mean, I did want the kiss to happen. But I wasn't planning for it to get—"

When his words awkwardly trailed away, she finished the sentence for him.

"So heated?"

Nodding ruefully, he blew out a heavy breath. "Now you're probably thinking I'm just a guy after sex."

She slanted him a droll look. "Hmm, well, now you're probably thinking I'm a sex-starved divorcée out to grab what excitement I can."

Shaking his head, he tried to keep a grin off his face, but it came anyway. "Never would I think something like that."

Through lowered lashes, she studied him closely. "And I don't believe you'd spend two hours with a pair of kids just to get a hot kiss from their mother."

His expression sobered. "I wouldn't say that. The kiss was worth every minute."

A nervous little laugh escaped her before she rose from the couch and walked over to where the remote for the television was resting on an end table. After she switched off the power, she returned to the couch to stand in front of him.

"I can't play coy, Denver. That's just not me. So I'll just come out and admit that I'm very attracted to you. I have been from the very first evening we met. I don't know what that means—for either of us. But I had to be open with you. So if you're wanting to run for the door right now, go ahead. I'll understand."

Caught off guard by her admission, he pushed himself up from the couch and reached for her hand. When her fingers willingly closed around his, he felt a fateful sort of acceptance wash through him.

"Since you're being honest, I'll admit that asking you for a date had very little to do with Rafe and Lilly. I wanted to spend this time with you. But I—"

"You planned on it being just this once."

As his gaze sheepishly roamed her face, he realized he was dealing with a woman unlike any he'd met before. She seemed to be reading his thoughts as though she could see right through his head. The idea left him feeling extremely exposed and vulnerable. Could she also see how fast his heart was racing? How much he wanted to pull her back into his arms?

"Well, maybe. I'm not a dating type of guy. And I don't want a serious relationship. But I thought one date wouldn't hurt anything—or maybe two. Now I see my thinking wasn't fair to you." Her brows arched in question, prompting him to go on. "What I'm trying to say is you deserve someone better than me."

"Yes, I do," she agreed, her voice edged with a mix of disappointment and determination. "So do my children."

He blew out another long breath and forced himself to drop his hold on her hands. Losing physical contact with her affected him in a way that didn't make sense. He hardly knew this woman. He didn't need to be that connected to her. Yet touching her made him feel alive and whole. Two things he hadn't really felt since Christa died.

"I agree. So I guess we should probably say goodnight and goodbye."

Her nostrils flared, and then her gaze flickered away

from his to settle on some shadowy spot across the room. "Is that what you want to do?"

Her voice was strained, as though there was an emotional cost to ask the question. Denver wanted to kick himself. He should've never touched or kissed her. After telling Harry and Peter good-night, he should've thanked her for the great dinner and then made a beeline back to the Silver Horn—where he belonged. Instead, he'd acted on his urges and now everything was changed.

"Not exactly. I'm just trying to do the right thing. For you and the boys."

Turning away from him, she walked over to where Mabel and Gus were still curled together in their basket.

"The boys like you. A lot. I could say that if you're trying to do the right thing, then you might think about coming around to see them once in a while. But that would be emotional blackmail and I don't want your company that way."

She turned around and gave him a fatalistic smile. "Sometimes being attracted to each other just isn't enough."

Something was suddenly pushing against his back, forcing his legs to carry him across the room to her.

"Common sense tells me to tell you goodbye and walk out the door. But that's not what your kiss told me. I think we'd both be fools to ignore what this chemistry between us really means."

Rolling her eyes, she let out a helpless groan. "It means you're a man and I'm a woman. It's that simple."

He frowned. "Really? Well, I don't go around wanting to kiss just any woman the way I just kissed you. Do you want to kiss just any man the way you kissed me?"

The corners of her lips turned downward. "That's not a fair question. Besides, why are you making this argument? You don't want to start up any sort of relationship with me."

"I didn't think I wanted to," he admitted as he rested his hands on her shoulders. "Until a few minutes ago and I was faced with the reality of never seeing you and the boys again."

She sighed. "So what if we do continue to see each other? Where could that possibly lead us? We'd only end up hurting each other. And I'd hate that."

"So would I. But we're mature adults. We've both been married. If things aren't working out with us, I think we have enough sense to end things long before one of us ends up with a broken heart. Don't you?"

She hardly looked convinced, and for a moment Denver thought she was going to tell him to get lost. Instead, she stepped forward and rested her palms against the middle of his chest. Her nearness had every cell in his body screaming to pull her even closer, to kiss her lips and throat, to wrap his fingers around her red hair and hold her head fast to his.

"No. I don't believe any of that," she answered. "But I'm going to pretend that I do. Because the idea of never seeing you again is—well, very unacceptable to me."

If Denver was a smart man, he'd be running backward right about now. And he wouldn't stop running until he was out of the house and away from the sight of her. At the very least, he should be flooded with fear. Instead, he was overwhelmed with happy excitement.

"I'm glad, Marcella. I like you and your sons very much. And it's been a long, long time since I've had a connection with a woman. One that makes me feel good."

"I'm glad, too." The soft smile tilting the corners of her lips turned impish. "So now that you've decided to stay, let's go to the kitchen. I'll make us some coffee while we clean up the rest of the dinner mess."

"Sounds good."

She curled her hand around his, and as they started to the kitchen, Denver wondered if he'd just made the best decision of his life, or become the biggest fool in the state of Nevada.

"Exactly who is this cowboy who's put these stars in your eyes?"

The question came from Marcella's mother, Saundra. At fifty-three, she was still youthful-looking with strawberry blond hair that brushed the tops of her shoulders and blue eyes similar to Marcella's. Careful attention to her diet maintained a slim figure, while equal dedication to skin care had kept most of the wrinkles at bay. But Saundra Benson's appealing surface hid a very contrary demeanor.

Ignoring the tinge of sarcasm in her mother's voice, Marcella sat down on the side of the bed and watched her pull a clean uniform from the closet. The thick knit dress of burgundy and pink could never pass for attractive and Saundra hated it, but so far she hadn't managed to get the restaurant to change the uniform just to please her.

Sighing, Marcella said, "Denver is more than a cowboy, Mom. He's a ramrod. He oversees the whole cow/calf operation on the Silver Horn. In case you didn't know, that's a huge ranch. The biggest in Nevada."

Saundra sat down on a dressing stool and began to pull on a pair of panty hose. "That's nice, dear. But you don't know anything about cowboys. They're coarse and uneducated. Most of them hardly have good table manners. Why would you possibly want to associate yourself with a man of that caliber?"

And why would you want to go out with a cheap tire salesman who uses bad grammar and wears garish ties? Marcella wanted to ask. Biting back the tart question, she said, "Denver isn't like anything you're describing. And how would you know about cowboys, anyway?"

With a mocking little laugh, Saundra stood and adjusted the panty hose at her waist. "Honey, I ought to know about them. I serve them every day. They either mumble or talk obnoxiously loud. Now, if you're actually wanting to find a good man, Marcella, I have several I've been keeping my eye on for you. The main one being a loan officer at Nevada Bank and Trust. He's very clean-cut and always wears three-piece suits. Nice ones. And he eats the same thing every day for lunch. Grilled cheese on rye. What could you possibly have against that?"

Marcella didn't have time for her mother's nonsense. Denver would be picking her up at seven this evening after she finished a split shift at the hospital. She needed to make arrangements for a babysitter before she left for work. "Sounds dangerous. I might die of excitement if I went out with him."

Saundra shot her a droll look. "All right, smarty, I'm sure you'd like cleaning cow manure off your heels better."

"Actually, it would be more interesting." She glanced at her watch. "I have to go, Mom. I need to be at the hospital in thirty minutes. Look, if you'd rather not keep Harry and Peter tonight, I can make other arrangements. Geena is always wanting the boys to come over and stay with her and Vince and baby Emma."

Saundra tugged the knit uniform over her head before she turned a frown on Marcella. "Geena has enough on her plate with taking care of little Emma Rose and new baby George. I'll watch my grandsons. Will they be staying overnight?"

Marcella walked to the door of her mother's bedroom. "I don't plan on being out that late, but I'm sure the boys are expecting to sleep over. You know how much they like having your French toast for breakfast."

"Fine," she said. "At least I won't be spending my Saturday night alone."

Marcella impatiently shook her head. "Mother, you're always trying to find me a man. You're still young and attractive. Why don't you put all that effort into finding someone for yourself? And I'm not talking about just for one or two dates. I mean someone to spend the rest of your life with."

Sighing, Saundra stood in front of the dresser mirror and adjusted the uniform until it fell to a spot just above her knees. "You know me, honey. I can attract a man, but I can't keep one."

"And we both know why."

Saundra grimaced at her own image. "Listen, Marcella, I don't want to spend my life biting my tongue or taking orders from a man. I have one boss. I don't want two. Besides, look who's talking about having a husband. You made a giant mistake marrying Gordon and wasted years trying to get past it."

Even though her mother's assessment of her was probably correct, Marcella didn't have time to discuss an issue that had been beaten to death over the years.

"I'm trying to get past it now," Marcella reasoned. "Now I've got to go. I'll walk the boys down about six thirty."

She was halfway down the hallway when her mother's head popped around the bedroom door.

"Marcella! Are you telling me you're getting serious about this cowboy?"

Was she? For the past week Marcella had been telling

her heart to be cautious and smart. She'd been assuring herself that she wasn't about to let herself become totally captivated over a man she was just now beginning to know. Yet the more time she spent with Denver, the more she longed to be with him.

"It's far too soon to be asking me that question."

Saundra snorted. "I married your father two weeks after I met him."

"Yes, and where is he now?" Before her mother could make a retort to that question, Marcella left the house and hurriedly walked the two short blocks to her own house.

Later that night, in a little Mexican café on the outskirts of the city, Marcella sipped her drink while silently chiding herself for ordering a margarita. Sitting across the intimate table from Denver was enough to tilt her senses without adding tequila to the mix.

"I'm really surprised that Harry and Peter didn't want to come along tonight. Did I make them angry or something?"

When Denver had called about going out tonight, his plan had been to take the three of them to a G-rated movie and out for fast food. But for some reason Harry and Peter had insisted they wanted to spend the evening with their grandmother. A decision that Marcella still found very suspicious.

Now the two of them were sitting in this tiny cantina with little more than a fat candle lighting their table and flamenco music playing softly in the background. The rich food on her plate was delicious, and so was his company.

"Harry and Peter are definitely not angry at you. In fact, they both made me promise to tell you hello and they'd see you next time. They're still talking about the picnic and the golf. And they're especially talking about you. I think they believe you're wearing a big *S* underneath your Western shirt."

Last weekend, Denver had taken the four of them on a picnic to Washoe Lake, then wrapped up the day back in Carson City with a round of miniature golf. The boys had been so thrilled with the outing they were still talking about it. As for Marcella, that halcyon day had been like a dream, one that she'd never wanted to end.

A wry smile on his lips, Denver dipped a corn chip into a bowl of avocado dip. "Well, I would've sworn they had a good time last weekend. But sometimes kids are good at hiding their feelings. Maybe they just pretended to be having fun to be nice to me."

Marcella laughed. "Now, that is funny. That trip to Washoe was thrilling for them. In fact, I'm betting they're probably getting it on their mind to beg you to take them camping. Just a warning, so you can have an excuse ready."

"Would they like to go camping? I remember Harry asking me if I knew how to fish."

Marcella smiled wanly. "They've never gotten to go camping before. Except for camping in the backyard. I bought them a tent and a bit of outdoor gear for that. I know it's not the same, so sooner or later I'm going to have to make good on my promises to take them on a real camping adventure."

He shook his head with disbelief. "I can't believe the boys haven't been camping. Your ex has never offered to take Harry, at least?"

She let out a short, cynical laugh. "Are you kidding? What he knows about camping you could put in your eye. And even if he was familiar with the outdoor pastime, he wouldn't offer. He lives in another part of the state and doesn't even bother to acknowledge Harry's birthday or ever see him."

"What a loss," Denver murmured.

"The man is clueless as to what he's missing." She sighed as she scooped up the last bite of enchilada with her fork. "But he does pay his child support—to avoid doing jail time."

A few moments of silence passed as both of them resumed eating. Then finally Denver spoke in a quiet voice, "Well, as much as I like Harry and Peter's company, I'm grateful to have you to myself tonight."

Marcella glanced over to see that his dark gaze was making a slow survey of her face, and suddenly she was reliving those few passionate moments on the couch when he'd kissed her. Since then, he hadn't tried to kiss her again and Marcella could only guess as to the reason. True, the children had accompanied them last weekend. But there had been a few occasions when the two of them had been alone long enough to exchange a kiss. It hadn't happened, and she was beginning to wonder if Denver had decided the two of them would be better off simply being friends.

But he wasn't looking at her like a friend. And whenever she gazed back at him, she certainly wasn't feeling friendly. Every inch of her was feeling like a woman.

"Yes, it's nice being able to talk. Just the two of us. The only time I get that is when I'm at work. And the conversation there is generally of a different kind—about injuries and wounds and treatments, living and dying. It gets pretty stressful at times."

He shook his head. "I don't know how you deal with it," he said admirably. "I couldn't."

"I've been trained to deal with it," she said easily. "Just

like you've been trained to do your job on the ranch. I couldn't rope a bull or deliver a calf."

"I wouldn't say that. There are plenty of women ranchers who can do those things. Like Sassy and Evan Calhoun's wife, Noelle."

The mention of the two Calhoun women had her casting him an impish smile. "Sassy and Noelle are exceptions. They not only know their way around a cattle pen, they do it all with a baby on their hip."

"That's true. Evan and Noelle's son, Little Bart, is only about seven months old," Denver said.

Before she could stop it, a wistful sigh slipped past her lips. "I got to see Little Bart at the Halloween party. He's so cute. I'd love to have another little boy to go with my two. Surprisingly, my guys are crazy about my friend Geena's baby girl. They'd love to have a sister. But... that's just a dream."

He leveled a sober look at her, and for a moment Marcella got the impression she'd said something wrong. But that didn't make sense. She'd only been talking about babies.

"So you'd like to have another child?" he asked stiffly.

She grimaced. "The way you ask that—well, you sound like I've shocked you."

His gaze dropped to his plate. "You already have two boys and they're half-grown. I'm just surprised that you'd want to start over with a baby."

"Well, hang on to your fork so you won't drop it. But I want more than one more baby. I'd love to have two or three more. I'm only thirty-three. So I have enough fertile years left. But I'm sure that dream will never happen," she conceded, then added with an awkward laugh, "No man wants to take on two half-grown boys, much less add three more to the family."

Thick black lashes partially hid his brown eyes as he glanced over at her.

"Is having a big family something you've always wanted?"

Reaching for her drink, she nodded. "When Spence and I were just little kids, I would beg our mother for another sister or brother. Then our parents got divorced and Dad moved to California. Losing him really hurt, and in my child's mind I kept thinking he would've never left if I'd had lots of brothers and sisters. That maybe just the two of us weren't enough for him. Of course, a dozen kids wouldn't have kept my parents together. But I never lost the desire for a big family. Maybe that's because I've never had a whole one. What about you?"

He dunked another corn chip into the creamy avocado, and though he appeared casual and relaxed, Marcella got the feeling the talk of family had made him more than uncomfortable.

That shouldn't surprise you, Marcella. The man is a widower. He's already told you he isn't in the market for a wife and family. He probably feels like you've thrown a pack of cigarettes onto the tabletop and shone a bright light in his eyes.

She was about to tell him he didn't have to answer her question when he said, "I never really thought about having a bunch of kids. I guess I was always too busy making a living for me and my wife. Then after she died—well, none of it really mattered."

"I probably shouldn't ask, but how did your wife die? An accident?"

His gaze slipped to a spot across the room where a man was sitting alone at the end of the bar. Marcella noticed that the beer drinker's expression looked as stark as Denver's.

Denver said, "She developed diabetes—a severe case. Over time she quit following doctor's orders and died of complications."

"It's an unforgiving disease."

"Yes. I learned exactly how unforgiving," he said, his voice tinged with bitterness.

The glow of the candlelight etched his rugged features with a soft gold color, and as Marcella studied his face, she wondered about the woman he'd loved and married all those years ago. In spite of her untimely death, she'd been a very lucky woman. At least for a little while.

She took another sip of her drink in hopes it would ease the thickness in her throat. "Life is short and unpredictable," she said gently. "Sometimes it doesn't turn out the way we plan or hope it will. Mine has certainly thrown me plenty of curveballs."

"Yes," he murmured. "We have to move on. Whether we want to or not."

She wasn't sure if he was talking about losing his wife or simply life in general. Either way, she wasn't going to push or prod him to open up old scars. She wanted this night to be easy and special for both of them.

Smiling brightly now, she said, "Tell me about your parents' ranch. What was it like for you growing up there?"

A glow of pleasure returned to his eyes and the sight of it filled her with relief. She wanted Denver to be happy. As happy as he'd made her and the boys.

"It was the best place in the world. For me, at least. Lots of cattle on wide-open spaces with plenty of horses to ride and dogs and cats for buddies. My parents had to work very hard to make ends meet, but they always made sure my sister and I had the things we needed."

"You got along well with them?"

"I adored Mom and Dad. Still do. They taught me so much. Not just about ranching but about becoming a man, owning up to my responsibilities and keeping a strong work ethic."

"Hmm. It makes me wonder why you're not still there. Working the ranch with your father."

A wry smile touched his lips. "Trust me, Marcella. If the Yates ranch had been big enough for the both of us, I'd still be there. But it's a small operation. Just big enough to support one family. I needed to get out on my own."

"I understand. So do you go back very often to visit?"

"Twice a year," he said with a regretful shake of his head. "Now that my parents are getting older, I keep promising myself to go more often. But it seems like we're always swamped on the Horn and I hate to leave Rafe shorthanded."

"Yes, that's the way it is with me. I wish I could go see my grandparents more often, but work doesn't allow me enough time to leave town."

She placed her drink back on the tabletop and Denver gestured to her plate. "If you're finished, we ought to be leaving. The movie will be starting soon and we're at least twenty minutes away from the theater."

Nodding, Marcella removed the napkin from her lap and reached for the handbag she'd placed under her chair. "Yes, I'm finished."

He motioned for the waitress, and while he took care of the bill, Marcella made a quick trip to the ladies' room. Minutes later, they stepped out of the restaurant to be greeted by a strong north wind and a spattering of rain.

"I have my hat to keep me dry. You stay here under the porch entrance and I'll pull the truck around," he told Marcella.

"I won't melt. Let's go!" Laughing, she grabbed his

hand and tugged him off the old wooden porch and across the graveled parking lot to his truck.

By the time he unlocked the doors and they hurriedly climbed inside, Marcella's face was wet.

"Oh, the rain is cold!" she exclaimed, shivering and laughing at the same time. "I should've worn my heavier coat."

He started the engine and punched a button to warm their seats. "The heater will warm in a few minutes. You should've waited instead of running out into this weather."

Swiping strands of damp hair from the line of her vision, she tossed him a teasing glance. "What's the matter? You don't like having your date look like a drowned rat?"

He chuckled, and then suddenly his hands were cupped around her face, drawing it toward his.

A sigh barely had time to escape her parted lips before his mouth was covering hers in a warm, gentle search that quickly had her wanting more.

"You look like a beautiful redheaded water nymph," he murmured against her cheek. "Raindrops taste very good on your skin—your lips."

As soon as the last word was out, he was kissing her again. This time the exploration was far deeper, and the flood of heat washing through her body instantly chased away her shivers.

Gravitating to the warmth of his hard body, she moved closer and wrapped her arms around his neck while her upper body strained to lean across the console and press itself to his.

Her response had him leaning into her, sliding his hands to the center of her back. His tongue probed at the edge of her teeth and she opened her mouth to him. The intimate contact splintered her senses and filled her with a craving she'd never felt before.

The kiss was still going when headlights suddenly flashed through the back windshield. The bright glare caused them to jerk apart as though a firecracker had exploded at their feet.

Her heart hammering, Marcella straightened around in the seat and gulped in several long breaths. Across from her, Denver mouthed a curse under his breath and jerked the truck into gear.

As he drove out of the parking lot, he said, "Sorry about that, Marcella. I— There for a minute, I…sort of forgot where we were."

"So did I." She glanced over at him and wondered what he was possibly thinking about her, wanting from her. Had that kiss implied he wanted to deepen their relationship? The mere idea of that rattled her as much as the kiss. "I don't know about you, Denver, but I'm not really in the mood for a movie."

Braking at a stop sign, he glanced over at her. "I'm not, either. So what would you like to do? The night is still early."

"It's rainy and cold. Why don't we just go to my place? I'll make us some hot chocolate and we can watch TV— or something."

"Are you sure? If there's something else you'd rather do, just tell me. I don't want this to be a bum date for you."

"Just spending time with you will be special."

An odd expression flickered across his face, and for a moment she thought he was going to insist they do anything besides what she was suggesting.

But then he shrugged one shoulder and turned the truck in the general direction of her house.

was long gone, yet the bareness of her lips made them even more appealing. Just looking at the moist curves caused his gut to clench with longing.

"It's certainly getting cold enough to snow. If that happens, we'll have to round up a huge herd of cattle off Tumbleweed Butte and bring them down to a more sheltered range."

"I don't know anything about ranching," she confessed, "but wouldn't that be something you'd do before bad weather arrived?"

He nodded. "Normally that's the case. But this autumn we decided to leave them on the butte a little longer because warm weather lingered and the grass was still good. Whether the snow comes tonight or later, we'll have to move them soon."

She pulled off her dress boots and, after squaring around on the cushion, drew her feet up under her. Tonight she was wearing a midnight blue dress made of some sort of knit that clung to her body like his leather work gloves shaped to his hands. She looked ravishing and sexy, and his palms itched with the want to touch her, to glide his hands over her curves and down the smooth, silky length of her legs.

"I can see where the weather would cause you extra work," she said, then with a thoughtful tilt to her head added, "Actually, it causes us extra work in the ER, too. Car accident victims, falls on the ice, skiing mishaps, frostbite. The list goes on and on. But in spite of the extra work, I enjoy seeing the mountains covered in white."

"Do you ski?" he asked.

She chuckled. "On the baby slopes. I took Peter and Harry skiing for a day last year at one of the resorts near Tahoe. As a Christmas gift from me. I think I fell far more than they did." Still smiling, she asked, "What about you? Do you ski or do outdoor sports?"

He shook his head. "Not winter sports. Unless you consider riding a horse up and down a snowy mountain a sport," he said wryly. "But I played lots of baseball in my younger years."

"Were you good at it?"

He shrugged. "Good enough to get a college scholarship."

"Wow, that's impressive."

"I suppose it was, but I turned it down."

Frowning, she studied his face, and Denver was suddenly imagining how different things might have been if he'd met Marcella all those years ago. Maybe his life would've taken a totally different path. Maybe he'd be a husband and father now. Instead of a widower.

"But why? That would've been a great opportunity."

He placed his empty mug next to hers on the coffee table. "That's true. But I didn't have any interest in trying to make a career out of baseball. My heart was already set on ranching. So I got an associate's degree in ranch management and played baseball just for the fun of it."

"Well, I'd better not let the boys know you were that good at the game. They'd never quit bugging you about it."

When he and Christa had first married, he'd had plenty of dreams about having sons and teaching them about baseball, ranching and all the things they'd need to know to become an adult. But then Christa had become ill and all hopes of having their own biological children had been stolen away. Now he tried not to picture himself with a family. He couldn't live through that kind of loss again.

"I noticed the boys had baseball gear in their bedroom. Do they do Little League?"

"Yes. With my work hours, it's not always easy to get to their games and practices, but I manage to attend most of them. Whenever work does interfere, I have a generous girlfriend who takes them along with her own boy."

As he studied her face, he realized the glow in her eyes had nothing to do with the nearby lamplight. The shine in her eyes was that of a mother talking about her children.

"It's not easy being a single parent, is it?"

One of her brows arched as though his question had surprised her. "So you've noticed."

"I've noticed. Along with a few other things." He looked across the room at the television Marcella had turned on earlier, but with the sound lowered it was little more than flickering colors and lights. Not that he would have paid any attention to what was happening on the screen. All he could think about was her warm body only inches away, her giving mouth and gentle hands. "It's very quiet without Harry and Peter here."

"I can't remember the last time I was home without them." Brushing her long hair back over her shoulder, she cast him a sheepish smile. "I shouldn't admit this to you, but I have the feeling they insisted on going to their grandmother's tonight just so that the two of us could be alone."

He stared at her. "What makes you think that?"

Her cheeks suddenly bloomed a rosy color. "Because they love spending time with you. They wouldn't have missed the chance unless—well, I think they've decided to play matchmakers. I hope you won't let it bother you. Believe me, it was none of my doing."

"Hmm. So you think they like the idea of the two of us together?"

"Far too much," she murmured. "But they—they're just kids—they don't understand about adults. I mean, about a man and a woman. Like me. And you."

Suddenly he couldn't stop himself from leaning toward her. "Well, I understand it. So do you. And I figure it's about time we did something about it. Don't you?"

"Denver."

She whispered his name as she moved toward him, and then he was gathering her in his arms, covering her lips with his.

Kissing her in the truck had been a quick, reckless impulse. This time was different. They were completely alone with no one to interrupt. And he intended to make the most of the opportunity.

With a needy groan, he shifted her upper body across his left arm, while his mouth settled more deeply over hers. Almost instantly her lips parted and the tip of her tongue invited his to slip inside. She tasted like crushed berries. Tart and sweet at the same time. And he couldn't get enough. Even when his lungs began to burn for oxygen, he didn't want to break the contact.

Her arms were wrapped around his neck, her fingers threaded through the hair at the back of his head. The softness of her rounded breasts pushing against his chest spurred his need to have more than her mouth and the taste of her kiss.

Before he could stop himself, he was guiding her down on the couch and shifting his body so that he was lying next to her. She welcomed the more intimate position by draping her body tightly over him and fastening her hands over the ridge of his shoulders.

Her reaction fueled his desire, and though it was impossible to deepen the fusion of their mouths, he tried. Until the desperate need to breathe had him tearing his lips away from hers and burying his face in the side of her hair.

"Marcella. Touching you, kissing you, shouldn't feel this good," he whispered roughly. "But it does."

Her lips pressed against his neck, causing his eyes to close, his loins to tighten. If she had any idea what she was doing to him, she would stop, he thought. Or would she? Maybe she wanted this as much as he did. The idea was like an accelerant to a fire that was already raging.

"Yes. So good," she murmured. "So perfect."

With his hand cupped around her chin, he brought her lips back to his, but the precious contact wasn't enough to satisfy either of them. He needed to touch her bare skin, slide his lips over her breasts and sink himself into the most intimate part of her.

Urgently his hand searched for the hem of her dress. Once he found it, he shoved the material upward, exposing the curve of her thigh and a portion of black panty covering her hip. As his hand explored the tender flesh, her mouth opened wider; her tongue begged for his.

Even though their bodies were already crushed tightly together, he tried to draw her closer. He wanted to feel the beat of her heart hammering against his. He needed the warmth of her flesh to chase away the cold shadows that had haunted him for so long.

Somewhere beyond the roaring in his head, he heard her moan, and the pleading sound fed the flames licking at his brain. He wanted this woman and she wanted him. That was all that mattered for now.

His hand moved to her inner thigh, and her legs parted. The invitation staggered him and suddenly the reality of the moment hit him so hard his eyes flew wide-open.

She doesn't want just sex on the couch. She wants babies and a husband. She wants a family!

The terrifying voice going off in his head was enough to have him jumping to his feet and grabbing up his hat.

"Denver! What— Are you leaving?"

He looked over to see her rising from the couch and smoothing her dress back over her hips. The sight caused him to shiver with lingering desire and a fear he couldn't shake.

With both hands curled around the brim of his hat, he forced himself to stand where he was until she reached him.

"I'm sorry, Marcella. I have to go. Now. You're not ready for this. I'm not ready for it. And I—" Drawing in a shaky breath, he practically coughed up the next words. "I'm not sure I ever will be."

Her face a picture of confusion, she wrapped her fingers over his forearm. "Denver—

"Don't ask me to explain, Marcella. I can't. It's not you. It's me."

He turned and headed to the foyer with her close on his heels. It was all he could do to keep from turning and lifting her into his arms. From carrying her straight to the bedroom and making love to her until the world around them was blotted away and nothing else mattered.

"I'm sorry, Denver. For me. For you. For the both of us," she said hoarsely.

"So am I, Marcella. More than you'll ever know."

Before she could touch him or say anything else, he opened the door and stepped out into the night.

The wind had picked up, and as he lifted his face to the dark sky, he saw bits of white snow dancing in the air.

Thank God he'd be spending long hours in the saddle on Tumbleweed Butte tomorrow, he thought. Maybe the arduous job would help to push Marcella from his aching heart.

* * *

"Marcella, have you gotten your flu shot? It's getting on down in November and we've already seen several cases in the ER."

The question came from Paige as the two women ate their evening meal in the hospital cafeteria. For the past ten minutes Marcella had stared at the chicken casserole on her plate rather than eat it.

Frowning, Marcella said, "Yes. I got the shot over a month ago. Why do you ask?"

"These past few days you've looked pale and droopy. I'm wondering if you're coming down with the flu or something."

"Or something" was more like it, Marcella thought grimly. Three whole days had passed since her date with Denver Saturday night. She hadn't heard from him since, and though she told herself he'd probably been busy dealing with the cattle and blizzard-like weather, she knew he'd had the time to text her, at least. But he hadn't and she didn't know what to make of his silence.

"I'm not getting ill, Paige. But I am miserable," she confessed. "And to make matters worse I haven't been able to hide my mood from Peter and Harry. They can tell that something is wrong with their mother, they just don't know what."

"Oh, what's happened? Did you get into an argument with your mother? Or is something wrong with your brother?"

A tight grimace flattened Marcella's lips. "I just heard from my brother a couple of days ago. He's fine. As for Mom, ever since she found out I was interested in Denver, she's been harping at me, swearing that all cowboys are irresponsible bums."

"How would she know? Did a cowboy break her heart at one time?"

"Not hardly. Since she and Dad divorced, she's never cared enough about any man to have her heart broken. No, I think Denver being a cowboy really has nothing to do with her opinion. She wants to pick out my dates. Not leave the choice up to the bad judgment of her daughter."

Paige groaned. "Oh Lord, Marcella, why do you let her opinion carry any weight with you, anyway? You're a grown woman with a mind of your own."

Marcella put down her fork and reached for her water glass. "In this case, I'm afraid she's right. I shouldn't have gotten involved with Denver."

Paige's mouth fell open. "Marcella, you can't be serious! I thought things with you two were heating up."

They'd heated up, all right, Marcella thought sadly. But Denver hadn't wanted any part of the fire, and she'd spent the past three days wondering what she'd done wrong. Why everything about his kisses had told her he'd wanted her, and then suddenly he hadn't wanted her. Just thinking about the abrupt way he'd left caused a heavy pain in the middle of her chest.

"I thought so, too. But we—uh, well, to be honest, I think Denver has decided he doesn't want to get involved. I mean, seriously involved. I haven't heard from him in a few days. I'm not even sure if I will."

Paige's head swung back and forth with disgust. "Men. They can be such bastards. Tell me, Marcella, why do we even want them around?"

Marcella sighed. "I often wonder. Then I see my friends with loving husbands and children and I can't help but hope and wish that I could have the same. But it's not going to happen with Denver. I can see that now."

Paige reached across the table and gave her hand a reassuring pat. "I'm sorry, honey. I was hoping you'd found the one," she said, then gave her a bright smile. "Maybe you have and he just doesn't know it yet? I know one thing, if you really care about the guy, I wouldn't give up on him. Some men need their arm twisted, you know."

"So why don't you give Dr. Sherman's arm a yank?" Marcella suggested. "You might wake him up."

Marcella expected her friend to make a sarcastic protest. Instead, Paige's expression turned somber. "I don't want to cause the man any more pain."

Paige's reaction momentarily distracted Marcella from her own problems. "What does that mean?"

Shrugging, Paige picked up a french fry but didn't bother lifting the piece of food to her mouth. "When someone needs to heal, you don't want to give them another wound—even if their bad behavior asks for it."

Marcella was still thinking about Paige's remark when she spotted Dr. Whitehorse entering the cafeteria. As she watched the tall, dark physician head over to the serving line, she wondered why he couldn't stir her body or touch her heart. He was handsome and easygoing and a dedicated professional. He'd make a wonderful husband and father, she decided. But he wasn't Denver. Damn it.

Glancing over her shoulder to see what had caught Marcella's attention, Paige spotted the good doctor. "Oh, there's the man you ought to be pursuing, Marcella. Everyone says he has his eyes on you. Why the heck don't you take advantage of it? Instead of mooning over a widower who's vowed to never marry again."

Jerking her gaze back to her plate, Marcella muttered, "I never said anything about Denver vowing to avoid marriage. I merely said he wasn't interested."

"Really, Marcella? Like there's a difference?"

Marcella was about to retort to Paige's well-meaning

sarcasm when she noticed Dr. Whitehorse heading in their direction.

She shot Paige a warning glance, then forced a cheerful smile on her face as the doctor paused next to their table.

"Good evening, ladies. How are things in the ER tonight?"

"An endless stream. The other nurses are going to be howling if we don't get back soon," Paige answered.

"How are things on your floor?" Marcella asked him politely.

"Not one empty room." A wry expression crossed his tanned features. "Sometimes I wonder why I chose internal medicine. I should've been an orthopedist or dermatologist. Now, those guys have time for a round of golf."

"Don't let any of them hear you say that," Paige joked.

A round of golf. Peter and Harry were still talking about playing miniature golf with Denver. And she was still remembering what a special time that day had been for her and her sons.

"Marcella, you're looking rather peaked this evening," the doctor commented. "Are you feeling okay?"

Paige said, "I asked her the same thing, Doctor."

Embarrassed that Dr. Whitehorse had noticed her dismal state, she did her best to smile at him. "Thanks for asking, Doctor, but I'm fine."

"Well, if you do start feeling ill, just come by my office upstairs," he offered. "You might need a prescription."

Marcella thanked him and after he'd said good-night and moved on to join a colleague at another table, Paige shot her a knowing look.

"And the prescription you need is him! He's dreamy, Marcella. And you two have everything in common. What do you and Mr. Cowboy have?"

Marcella grimaced as the image of Denver walking out the door took center stage in her mind. He'd been visibly anguished, and though his quick exit that night had left her wounded, she couldn't be angry at him. Instead, she felt defeated and very, very sad for Peter and Harry.

Sighing, she rose to her feet and picked up her tray. "I don't know if I have anything with him, Paige. That's something I need to figure out."

The office Denver shared with Rafe was a dusty, cluttered room with two wooden desks facing each other and a row of metal filing cabinets lining one wall. A pair of windows looked out of the cattle barn and across a portion of the ranch yard, which this morning was decorated with a measurable amount of snow that had fallen the night before.

Since he and Rafe both hated the business side of ranching, the men spent as little time as possible sitting at their desks. But this morning, Denver was forcing himself to deal with feed and vaccination orders.

"Denver, I think we'd better have a couple of hands count the alfalfa bales in the small barn. This morning after the men loaded the hay truck it's starting to look pretty empty."

Denver glanced away from his computer screen to see that Rafe had left his desk and was standing at a nearby table pouring himself a cup of coffee. Even though it was only a few minutes after nine, both men had already saddled up and ridden five miles out to check a herd of yearling calves that was impossible to reach by vehicle. The cold ride had left Rafe's face red with windburn, and seeing it reminded Denver of how devoted his friend was to the ranch. A man as wealthy as Rafe didn't have to do such menial chores. He could have sent someone in his place, but Rafe wanted to see the cattle's condition for himself. Not through another man's eyes.

"Already?" Denver asked. "We just had that barn filled a month ago."

Rafe sipped the hot drink before he replied, "I know. But the antelope and deer are hungry, too. And with snow on the ground, they're eating as much hay as the cattle."

"There's not much we can do about that."

Rafe shook his head. "No. And I wouldn't want to. I don't want to think of any animal going hungry."

Denver nodded. "I'll have Frank and Leo make a bale count. In the meantime, I'll check to see if we have any hay scheduled to arrive soon. We might have to supplement the alfalfa with timothy until we can have more shipped."

"Hmm. That would cut down on the protein. We'd have to increase the grain feed. I'll talk to Dad and have him see what he can locate in the way of alfalfa."

"Good idea," Denver told him. "I'll have the guys make a count of the timothy bales while they're at it."

He started to turn back to the computer screen when the cell phone on his desk vibrated with the alert of a text message.

Annoyed for the interruption, he started to ignore the notification, then decided it might be some of the hands texting for help.

Once he scrolled to the new message, his jaw practically dropped to see the sender was Marcella. Is there any way you can come to town today? I need to see you.

Had something happened to her? Or the boys? He couldn't bear to let his mind go in that direction.

"You're scowling, Denver. Is anything wrong?"

He glanced up from the phone to see Rafe approaching

his desk, and from the concerned frown puckering his forehead, he'd already guessed that something was amiss.

"Uh—no. I don't think so," Denver told him. "It's Marcella. She says she needs to see me. I haven't talked to her in a few days, so I'm at a loss as to what this is about."

Rafe made a grunt of disapproval. "Why haven't you talked with her? Aren't you two dating?"

Denver wiped a hand over his face. "Hell, Rafe, you make it sound like we're a pair of teenagers going steady and need to stay in constant contact."

"I'm hoping this is a steady thing with you two. Marcella couldn't be more perfect for you. And you'd be perfect for her—if you'd just let loose."

Let loose. He'd let go, all right, Denver thought ruefully. Another minute or two in Marcella's arms and they would have been making love. And that would've changed everything about their relationship. He wasn't ready for that. Or was he? These past few days he'd been aching like hell to see her again, to have her back in his arms.

With a heavy sigh, he placed the phone on the corner of his desk. "I don't want to get serious, Rafe. I can't give Marcella what she wants or needs."

"And what is that? If you're talking about money—"

Denver interrupted with a shake of his head. "Money has nothing to do with it—I have plenty of that. She wants babies. A family. I can't give her those things."

Rafe's brows lifted in question. "Why not? Are you sterile or something?"

Denver groaned with frustration. "No. It's nothing like that."

"Then—"

"I don't want to talk about it, Rafe."

"Well, all I can say is you'd better talk about it with Marcella. That is, if you care anything about her at all."

Years ago, when Denver first started working with Rafe and his family, he'd told them he was a widower and that his wife had died from diabetes. He hadn't gone into the details, though. At the time the whole tragic incident had been too painful to relate to anyone. Instead, he'd bottled away the heartbreak and tried to move on and forget. Unfortunately, the past always had a way of being linked to the future, and now it was rearing up to slap him in the face.

"I do care. I guess that's why...I want her to be happy. And—well, I'm not the man who can make her happy."

Rafe shook his head with disgust. "If that's the way you feel, then you ought to be up front with her. She doesn't need to be wasting her time on you."

Even though Rafe's assessment of the situation was correct, just hearing it cut Denver right to the core.

"You got that right," he said glumly.

Rafe glanced at his watch. "There's not much going on this morning. I want you to drive into town and go by the saddle maker's to see how he's coming on the new saddle I'm having made."

Denver bit back a curse. Giving Denver an excuse to drive into Carson City was ridiculous. This was all about Marcella and they both knew it.

"The saddle maker doesn't have a telephone?"

Rafe slanted him a pointed glance before heading back to his desk. "I can't see the tooling over the phone. I want you to look at it firsthand. That way you can give me your opinion on how it's shaping up."

"Just like you'd have the man tear the saddle apart and do the tooling over? Sure, Rafe," he said with a heavy dose of sarcasm.

"The money I'm paying for that saddle—you bet I would."

"And I'm sure you're thinking I'll have plenty of time to stop by Marcella's after I go by the saddle shop?" Denver asked wryly.

"Exactly. After all, how long does it take to tell a woman you're finished with her?"

Grim-faced, Denver rose to his feet. "Shut down my computer for me, would you? This might take longer than you think."

"Take your time," Rafe told him. "The ranch will be here when you get back."

Chapter Eight

How long did it take for a man to convince himself to give up the best thing he'd ever held in his hands? And where did he find the strength to be that unselfish? As Denver drove through the residential streets to Marcella's house, the questions rolled over and over in his mind. Yet the closer he got to her place, the more the answers evaded him.

Forty-five minutes ago, before Denver had left the ranch, he'd texted Marcella to let her know he was coming into town and would be stopping by to see her. As soon as he stepped onto the tiny porch, the door opened before he ever had time to knock. She must have been watching for him, he decided.

"Hello, Denver," she greeted. "Please come in."

"Hello, Marcella."

He walked past her, and while she fastened the door behind him, he noticed she was dressed in old jeans and a baggy black sweater. Obviously she wasn't going in to work anytime soon. Nor did she consider his visit a special event. Which was hardly surprising, considering the abrupt way he'd left the last time he was here, Denver thought ruefully.

"I hope you had another reason for making the drive to town today," she said as she gestured for him to precede her into the living room. "I didn't want you to make a special trip on my account."

Her voice was stilted, almost to the point of being distant, and Denver decided she was about to save him the difficult task of ending things between them. The notion should have filled him with immense relief. Instead, anger and helplessness were swirling through him, upending his rattled emotions even more.

He took off his hat and coat and placed them on the cushion of an armchair. "No problem. I had an errand to run for Rafe. And there's no urgent reason for me to rush back to the ranch. At least, not this morning."

She gestured for him to take a seat, and Denver sank into the same spot on the couch where their kissing session had started the other night. Whether he'd chosen to sit there out of a sense of familiarity or masochism, he didn't know. Either way, he found he couldn't tear his eyes off her or stop the runaway pounding of his heart.

She eased onto the edge of the cushion next to him and squared her knees so that she was facing him directly. Her back was ramrod straight, her lips compressed to a thin line. He'd never seen her in a mood like this before, and the revelation told him there was far more to sweet Marcella than he'd first imagined.

"I guess you've been wondering why I wanted to see you," she said flatly.

"At first I was worried that something might have happened to you or the boys," he admitted. "Now I can see that isn't the case."

"Sorry. I didn't mean to worry you. It's just that since you left the other night I've been doing a lot of thinking about you—us. And I wanted to— No, I need to explain some things before more time passes."

Her blue eyes were full of shadows and Denver felt like hell. He'd never planned to hurt her, but somehow he'd managed to take the sparkle from her eyes and smile from her face.

"Marcella, I'm sorry you haven't heard from me. I—"

"Forget it," she interrupted. "After it became clear you weren't going to bother calling, I've—well, like I said, I've been thinking—"

When her voice trailed away on an anguished note, he finished the sentence for her. "You don't want us to see each other anymore," he said bluntly. "Right?"

Shoving her loose hair away from her face, she momentarily closed her eyes, and as Denver studied her lovely image, he realized giving her up might be the right thing to do, but it was far from what he actually wanted.

She said, "I think it would be best. For you. Me. And the boys."

The mention of Harry and Peter pulled his brows together. "Am I missing something here? What does us not having sex have to do with the boys?"

Her expression incredulous, she stared at him. "You think sex, or the lack of it, is what I'm concerned about? That's the most inflated male ego remark I've ever heard."

"It wasn't a remark," he corrected. "It was a question. And what am I supposed to think? I understand you're angry with me for running out the other night. And yes, I should've already called or texted you, but I—well, I needed time."

He realized that sounded worse than feeble, but how could he explain the emotions that had been tearing him one way and another?

Why don't you try being completely honest with her,

Denver? Why don't you open up that scarred heart of yours and let her see what a mess you are?

Fighting against the bitter voice in his head, he refocused his attention on her face. At the moment her features were tight with anger. An emotion he'd never seen her display before.

"Time for what? To figure out whether you want me that much?" she asked curtly. "Well, in case you've forgotten, I have two boys who've already been hurt by selfish, indifferent men. I'm not going to let them continue to invest their emotions in you, and then you suddenly decide to disappear from their lives. I can't bear for them to be hurt like that. Not by you or any man."

He was trying not to be offended. Protecting her children was a huge part of being a good mother. But putting him in the same category as those loser dads ripped him right down the middle.

"So you think I'm that sort of man?" he asked.

Her sigh was heavy with frustration. "I wasn't comparing you to Harry's and Peter's worthless fathers. There's no comparison there. But surely you can see how my sons have grown enormously fond of you."

"And I've grown more than fond of them," he admitted. "I hope you can see that."

"I believe you feel that way. But with you and me— well, this morning at breakfast they begged me to ask you to come to dinner tonight. I didn't have the heart to tell them that you have some sort of hang-up about me and you won't be coming around—"

Her voice broke off with a strangled sound, and before Denver could stop her, she jumped to her feet and stood with her back to him.

He rose just as quickly, and though he wanted to pull

her into his arms, her rigid stance made him doubt she would welcome his touch.

Staring at the back of her head, he spoke gently, "Marcella, you don't understand. Just because you hadn't heard from me—I hadn't quit on us. I care about you and the boys. Very much." When she didn't respond, he placed his hands on her shoulders and tugged her around until she was facing him. "The other night when I left, you can't imagine how sick—how scared and stupid—I felt."

Her head swung back and forth in confusion. "The way you left, I could see how much you—well, I thought you suddenly realized you didn't want me."

Groaning helplessly, he wrapped his arms across her back and pulled her tight against him. "Oh, baby, I wanted you. So much. It was all I could do to get up and leave. But I…I've been telling myself if I wasn't so selfish, if I was any kind of man at all, I'd step aside and let you find a man worthy of you and the boys."

Tilting her head back, he could see dark turmoil swimming in her blue eyes.

"Denver, I remember in the beginning we both said we weren't looking for anything serious. But things started changing with me, and I thought maybe they were changing with you."

His hands roaming her back, he continued to hold her close, and the warmth of her body chased away the awful ache that had gnawed at him for the past few days.

"I've felt them changing, Marcella. That's why—" Taking hold of her hand, he urged her down on the couch. "Let's sit and I'll try to explain."

"About us?" she asked.

Her hand was still clinging to his and the warm connection helped him find the courage to go on.

"Before I get to us, I need to tell you about me. And

why I've gone all these years making sure I—" pausing, he drew in a deep breath "—never got close to a woman. I mean, emotionally close."

Her fingers tightened around his as though she understood exactly how much it was costing him to talk about a life he'd tried so hard to forget.

"Denver, you've already told me your wife died from a medical condition. That's enough—"

"No," he interrupted with a shake of his head. "It isn't enough. You need to hear how everything happened. Christa's death was senseless and I was so angry about it for such a long, long time."

"And now?"

His gaze dropped to their entwined hands. Her fingers were small and pale against his big brown hand, and he told himself that in spite of her fragile appearance she was strong and healthy. He wouldn't lose her like he lost Christa. No. He might lose her a different way. But not like that.

"I'm not angry anymore. I just want to make sure nothing like that ever happens again. That's why when I get close to you, when I think about making love to you, I get terrified."

Her gaze was roaming his face searching for answers.

"I don't understand, Denver. But I want to. Very much."

For a moment he closed his eyes and tried to gather the right words. But words couldn't paint the picture of pain and sadness he'd carried inside him for so long.

"All right, I'll go back to the very beginning," he said. "To when I left my parents' ranch in Moorcroft and took a ranching job near Laramie. That's when I met Christa. I was twenty at the time and she was eighteen. She was waitressing in a local café and going to college part-time."

Her features softened. "And the two of you fell in love."

He nodded. "After a few months we got married and lived in a little house provided by the ranch. We both wanted children right away, but we decided it would be best for Christa to finish her associate's degree before we took on the added responsibility of a baby."

"That was logical."

He grimaced. "Yes. We thought we had our future planned like two mature adults. We were willing to work hard and wait for things to fall into place."

"And then Christa developed diabetes," she said knowingly. "That must have hit you both pretty hard."

"It did. But the doctors told us if she stuck to the rules and took good care of herself, she could live a fairly normal life. So we both felt positive about her condition. Except there was one hitch in those rules and it was a big one. Attempting to carry a baby could put her life at risk."

Marcella nodded grimly. "Yes, in some cases of diabetes, depending on the severity, pregnancy is very risky. Hearing that warning was surely a huge disappointment for the both of you."

Denver grimaced. "It was a regrettable situation, but I wasn't going to let it ruin our plans for the future. As far as I was concerned, we could adopt the children we wanted. So I told Christa that one of us needed to permanently remove the chance of an unwanted pregnancy. Preferably me."

The corners of her mouth dipped downward. "I don't imagine that suggestion went over very well."

He shook his head. "She pleaded with me not to do anything drastic. She argued that her health might eventually improve enough to have a baby, or that medical science would advance enough to cure her. In the meantime, she promised she would faithfully remain on birth control."

"So you gave in to her wishes," she said perceptively.

Denver passed a hand over his face. "I couldn't take away her hope of someday being the mother of her own child."

"That would have been a heavy blow for a woman to take. Especially one as young as your wife," Marcella said with understanding.

"A heavy blow would have been better in the long run," he said bitterly. "At least she would have been alive."

She must have guessed what he was about to say next because her lips parted with dismay.

"You mean she went against her doctors' advice and broke her promise to you?"

"That's right. By the time she finished college she was feeling great, and without anyone knowing, including me, she quit taking her pills." He looked away and swallowed as the memories of that time surged up to choke him. "The pregnancy almost made it to the third trimester, but then things started going wrong and she and the baby both died."

Long moments of silence passed before she finally murmured, "How utterly awful."

Drawing in a long breath, he held both her hands tightly between his. "My family, my future, was wiped out completely," he said huskily. "I left the ranch where I'd been working. I couldn't bear living there anymore. That's when I moved here to Carson City and got a job on the Horn. The Calhouns saved me, so to speak. They took me in like family, and now twelve years later I'm happy to be where I am."

Her somber gaze traveled over his face and Denver was struck by the mist of tears he saw in her eyes. "Are you? Are you happy enough to push Christa's tragedy behind you? Or are you still in love with the young wife you lost?"

Marcella's last question caught him by surprise. Maybe because he'd never stripped it all down to such a simple approach to his feelings. "Why, no," he said after a moment. "I haven't been in love with Christa's ghost for all these years. I'm not even sure I was in love with her when she died."

The harsh intake of her breath had Denver casting her a rueful glance.

"Don't take that in the wrong way, Marcella. I loved Christa. And I desperately wanted her to live. I wanted us to have a future together. But I'll admit that when she deliberately deceived me about the pregnancy, it crushed something special between us and I was never able to get it back."

"Well, for some women the need to have a baby is so strong it dictates their reasoning. I'm sure in Christa's mind, she was telling herself everything would be all right. That your baby would be born healthy and the three of you would be happy. In the long run she wasn't really deceiving you by getting pregnant, Denver. She was deceiving herself. Pretending that she was just like any normal, healthy woman."

Bending his head, he drew his hands from hers and raked them through both sides of his hair. "A part of me knows that, Marcella," he mumbled. "And I've tried to forgive her, tried to forget and move on, but—"

Suddenly her hands were cupping his face, and when he lifted his head, the compassion he saw in her eyes was like a soothing balm, coating all the raw, rough edges of his heart.

"Oh, Denver, what happened to Christa isn't going to

happen to me. I'm healthy. Besides, I'm a nurse. I know not to put my health at risk. You have to forgive her and move on. Otherwise, there's no room inside you for me or any woman."

As he studied her sweet face, sudden resolve washed over him, and for the first time since Christa had died, he saw a different future for himself. It wasn't black or filled with loneliness. "Any woman? Oh, Marcella, I don't want just any woman. I want you. I've wanted you from the moment you walked into my dirty kitchen."

Smiling seductively, she moved closer and slipped her arm across his chest. As she leaned into him and whispered against his cheek, Denver realized his resistance had disappeared like a dust cloud on the desert.

"And I want you, Denver. More than you can imagine. We can make this work. Just give me the chance to show you."

Groaning with need, he pressed his lips to the corner of hers and wondered if she could actually show him how to love again.

"I'm all yours, darlin'," he murmured, then closed his lips over hers.

As Denver's kiss deepened to a hungry search, Marcella's senses began to float around the room and dance like starlight on a rippling lake. Everything was different now. She could feel it in the way his hands were touching her. The way his lips were kissing her with hot abandon. And she couldn't get close enough. Couldn't begin to satiate the need he was creating deep within her body, her very soul.

When he finally lifted his head enough for them to breathe, she whispered, "The bedroom."

His hands gently cradled her face. "Are you certain?"

Marcella didn't have to think about his question. From his very first kiss, her body had been screaming the answer. She wanted to be connected to this man in every intimate way.

"Completely certain," she said, placing her lips next to his. "And don't worry—I'm protected with the pill. And Nurse Marcella never forgets to take her medicine."

"I'm not worried about that. Not now."

"No?"

He answered her question by rising to his feet and lifting her into the cradle of his arms. As he carried her out of the room, she anchored her arms around his neck and tried not to wonder if he was carrying her to paradise or a broken heart.

You just told Denver you were certain about this. It's too late to start having second thoughts now, Marcella. It's time for you to be woman enough to make him forget about everything except wanting you.

By the time they entered the small bedroom and he set her on her feet at the side of the double bed, she'd pushed the words of warning from her mind. These past few days she'd decided there was little to no hope of them having a future together. Now here she was about to make love to him, and the idea was causing every cell in her body to throb with excitement.

Standing in the circle of his arms, with his lips continuing to feast on hers, she went to work releasing the snaps on the front of his shirt. At the same time, his hands delved beneath the hem of her baggy sweater and walked their way upward until they reached her breasts.

The fact that she wasn't wearing a bra must have shocked him, because for one split second she felt his hands hesitate before his fingers finally curled around her naked breasts. The contact of his rough skin against hers was both sweet and erotic, prompting her eyes to close and her body to arch into his.

Even through the heavy denim of his jeans, Marcella could feel his erection, and it sent a thrill of feminine triumph soaring through her. After years of not having a man in her life, she'd almost forgotten how exhilarating it felt to have someone want her this much. For her to want this much. Or had she ever really felt like this?

When his mouth finally tore away from hers, she knew the answer to that. She'd never had her senses spin so out of control that she had to keep telling herself to breathe. The taste of his lips, the scent of his skin, had whirled her into orbit and she didn't care if she ever returned to earth.

She was hardly aware of him tugging off her sweater or tossing it to the floor. But when his head dipped and his lips began to nuzzle both her breasts, she drew in a sharp breath and latched her hands tightly over the tops of his shoulders.

It wasn't until he'd taken one hard budded nipple between his teeth and laved it with his tongue that the pent-up air rushed from her lungs. And by then it didn't matter that her mind had ceased to think rationally. All she wanted was to have his hands moving over her body. To have him inside her, driving hard and fast.

When her fingers fumbled with his belt buckle, he swiftly pushed her hands aside and lifted his head. "Let me," he whispered. "It'll be faster."

Leaving him to handle the task, she focused on removing the remainder of her own clothing while he stripped down to nothing but a pair of white boxers. The lone garment was a vivid contrast against his dark skin, and though she didn't want to stare, she couldn't tear her gaze off his hard-muscled chest and arms, lean waist and long, sinewy legs.

When he finally turned to see her standing next to him wearing only a pair of black lace panties, he paused and let his gaze travel up and down the length of her.

"Wow, I was expecting you to look good, but not this good," he said, his voice thick with desire. "Perfect."

Considering the fact that she'd been celibate for so long, she'd expected to feel awkward about standing naked in front of this man. But oddly enough she felt no sort of embarrassment or need to hide from Denver's smoldering gaze. Her body was hardly perfect, but the sizzling glint in his eyes said she looked good to him. And that was enough. Just to please him and know that he wanted her and only her.

"I never realized you're half-blind. Lucky me," she said, a provocative smile tilting her lips. "You can't see what you're really getting."

Grinning, he reached for her, and as his lips made a hot foray over hers, Marcella was certain she was going to wilt with pleasure. Thankfully, just before her knees gave way, he lowered both of them onto the bed.

Once they were lying face-to-face in the middle of the mattress, he smoothed a hand down her bare arm and whispered, "My vision hasn't been this clear in years."

Marcella touched her fingertips to his cheek. Immediately he caught her hand and turned the palm up to his lips. The gesture caused her heart to swell and tears to sting her eyes.

"Denver, if you're concerned about…me getting pregnant, I won't mind if you want to use your own birth control. If that would make you feel better."

His brown gaze searched hers. "No. I don't want things to start out that way with us. I need to learn to trust again."

His admission brought a rush of moisture to her eyes. "I do, too," she murmured. "So we'll learn together."

"Together. I like the sound of that."

His hand began to roam the curve of her hip and down the slope of her thigh. The warm touch of his calloused palm sent shivers of anticipation over her skin. Her lips tilted upward at the corners.

"How long has it been since you made love to a woman in the middle of the morning?" she asked.

A chuckle rumbled from his throat. "Is that a trick question?"

Her soft laugh joined his as she snuggled her head beneath his chin. "I'm only teasing. Not trying to pry a confession from you."

"So you're a teaser, are you?" Pulling his head back slightly, he picked up a handful of her vibrant hair. "Where did that come from? All this red hair?"

Smiling slyly, she allowed her fingers to dance across his chest. "Mmm, could be. I have a few red hot chili peppers in me, too."

His hand slipped to the small of her back and pressed her even closer. "I'd better be careful," he whispered, his lips moving against her cheek. "I might get scorched."

"Don't worry. I'm a nurse. I can take care of your burns."

That brought another chuckle from him, and then his mouth was crushing down on hers, shooting her senses off in a thousand different directions.

The kiss went on and on until Marcella hardly knew if she was in her own bed or floating on a cloud with the hot sun sizzling over her skin, melting her into helpless puddles of flesh.

Desire that she'd never known existed inside her was rapidly spiraling out of control. It pushed her hands into a frantic search of his body and caused her hips to arch against his hard manhood.

The needy groan in her throat was close to being a whimper, and the sound caused him to lift his mouth from hers. His drowsy eyes were full of concern as they looked into hers.

"Am I hurting you?"

"Only because I want you so much. Make love to me, Denver," she pleaded. "Make the ache go away."

"Oh, Marcella. My sweet. Let me show you how much I want you. So much. Too much."

Rolling her onto her back, he quickly peeled off her panties and tossed them to the floor. Marcella watched, her body tingling with need as he slipped the boxers off his hips and allowed them to slide to the floor.

The sight of his hard arousal caused the ache between her legs to deepen, her breaths to quicken. When he finally positioned himself over her, she expected him to immediately connect their bodies. Instead, he delayed her torment by lowering his head until his tongue was tracing a wet circle around one nipple and then the other.

Marcella was on fire, every inch of her burning until she felt like a flame rising higher and higher. And then suddenly he was entering her, slowly, sweetly, until there was no space between them. Only hot flesh.

Somewhere through a fog of desire, she heard his guttural groan, and then he began to move, sending delicious waves of pleasure undulating from her head to her toes.

When she finally managed to catch her breath, she began to match the rhythm of his strokes. Their bodies melded perfectly and before long Marcella was totally lost in him and the moment. The only important thing was to try to give him all the incredible sensations he was giving her.

Forever. That was how long it would take for her to get enough of this man. She wanted to hold him to her like this until love had bound them together so tightly nothing could tear them apart.

As she clung to him, the thought continued to swirl in her subconscious. But that sweet forever place in her mind was suddenly interrupted as the pace of his body quickened and she recognized he was racing toward that same spot she was seeking.

They found that place together and for long, long moments Marcella felt sure a part of her was dancing on the ceiling and somersaulting through the bright sunlight streaming through the windows.

Even after her mind had settled back to its proper axis and her gasps for breath had slowed, her body was still wallowing in the delicious afterglow of his lovemaking. And though she welcomed his slack weight, he soon moved to one side and rested a forearm against his forehead.

"Nurse, am I still breathing?"

His murmured question had her reaching over and resting her palm upon his chest. The fast beat of his heart thumped against her fingers.

"I think so. But you're experiencing a rapid heartbeat." She rolled toward him until she was close enough to press a kiss against his damp cheek. He smelled like a man. Her man. And she couldn't get enough of the scent or the taste of his skin.

"What do you prescribe to fix it?" he asked. "Bed rest?"

"And lots of it," she answered impishly.

He turned his head toward hers and her heart swelled at the soft light she spotted in the brown depths of his eyes. It was like nothing she'd ever seen from him, or any man before, and though she wanted to believe it was love, she stopped her thoughts from going there. She was old enough and wise enough to know that one session of hot sex didn't equal love. And yet the soft, warm feelings in her heart were getting awfully close to it.

"How much time do you have before you head to the hospital?" he asked.

"A few hours," she answered, then asked, "How long until you need to get back to the Silver Horn?"

Groaning, he reached for her. "Long enough."

Marcella's lips found his, and as he begin to kiss her once again, she closed her eyes and told herself the needy feeling in the middle of her chest had nothing to do with her heart.

Chapter Nine

"Denver, you and Marcella and the boys are perfectly welcome to join us for Thanksgiving dinner here on the Horn," Rafe said to him as the two men walked across the ranch yard toward one of the ranch's many horse barns. "Greta always has enough food for a huge crowd. Besides, Dad and Grandfather will both be missing that day. Dad's going up to stay a few days with Finn and Mariah over the Thanksgiving holiday and Grandfather will be spending the day over at Evan and Noelle's. We need some more faces at the table."

"It's nice of you to offer, Rafe," Denver told him. "But I've already promised Marcella I would make dinner for her and the boys. And I don't want her to think I'm reneging."

Without breaking stride, Rafe looked quizzically over at him and laughed. "You making Thanksgiving dinner? I realize you can cook enough to keep meat on your bones, but a holiday feast is a bit different, Denver. Unless you've already warned Marcella that she and her sons will be eating sandwiches."

"Very funny," Denver said. "I'm not spoiled like you are—with a house cook and maids and a wife at your beck and call. I know how to cook and clean and do for myself. And since Thanksgiving is only three days away, I'd better start cleaning the kitchen tonight."

Rafe continued to chuckle. "Well, I'll admit I'm spoiled and it feels pretty good. So you do all that cooking and cleaning and save me a piece of pumpkin pie. I want to see how good of a pastry chef you are."

"I didn't say anything about making pastries," Denver countered. "I'll purchase those from the bakery in town."

"That's cheating," Rafe joked, then his expression sobered as he glanced over at Denver. "So how are things going with you and Nurse Marcella? Is she taking care of your aches and pains?"

A week and a half had passed since Denver had driven into town with intentions of ending things with Marcella. He'd expected that visit to be his last with her. Instead, that day had ended up being one of the most incredible of his life.

That morning, when he'd carried Marcella to her bedroom, he'd believed he was going to have sex with a sensual redhead. Instead, he'd ended up making love to the most beautiful, giving woman he'd ever known. The closeness they'd shared that day had changed him in ways he was still trying to understand.

"Do I look sick?" Denver retorted.

Rafe laughed out loud. "No. As a matter of fact, I've never seen you look better. Marcella must be doing something right."

Denver's sigh was lost on the cold wind swooping across the ranch yard. "She's a special woman, Rafe. Sometimes I wonder what the hell I'm doing."

The two men entered the cavernous barn and walked down a wide alleyway until they reached a large tack room filled with equipment the ranch hands used on a daily basis. Compared to the freezing temperature outside, the room felt blessedly warm, and after spending most of the day outdoors, Denver welcomed the relief.

"What does that mean?" Rafe asked. "I thought you'd gotten all that doubt stuff out of your system."

These past days, Denver and Marcella had spent as much time together as possible. A few occasions they'd spent alone; in other cases, the boys had been present. And each time he'd said goodbye and returned to the ranch, he'd felt a little of himself remaining behind with her and her sons.

"I'm working on it," he said flatly.

"Damn, Denver, what are you waiting on? For everything to be perfect? Everything to be guaranteed? Well, here's a news flash for you—life doesn't work that way. And another thing you ought to know—it doesn't stand still. You're wasting precious time."

His jaw set, Denver walked to the far side of the dusty room and pulled down several saddle cinches from a peg on the wall. Tossing them to the floor, he said, "These are no good. And there's several head stalls here with torn leather and broken bits. You want to give them away or send them to the saddle shop to be repaired?"

Rafe walked over to where Denver was standing. "Right now I'm not worried about a bunch of unusable tack. We'll deal with it in a few minutes. Right now I'm probably sticking my nose where it doesn't belong, but I want to know about you and Marcella."

"You're right," Denver said bluntly. "You are being nosy. Don't we have enough things to discuss without bringing up Marcella?"

"Okay, so I'm prying. But Lilly and I are the reason you got hooked up with Marcella in the first place. We sort of feel responsible for you two. Understand?"

With a rough sigh, Denver sat down on a wooden storage box. "Sorry, Rafe. I don't mean to sound short. It's just that—"

"That what?" Without waiting for an answer, Rafe pulled a rubber feed tub over in front of Denver and flopped it over to use as a makeshift seat. "Until a moment ago I thought things were going great for you two."

"They are going great. That's what worries me. I never meant for things with Marcella to get serious. But they're getting there. And I don't know what to do to stop it."

Rafe's head swung back and forth. "Why would you want to stop it? You could look for years and not find a woman of Marcella's caliber. You ought to be jumping for joy. Is the fact that she has a pair of boys putting you off?"

Rafe's question put a deep frown on Denver's face. "No. It makes her even more appealing. Harry and Peter are very special to me. But—well, like I told you, she wants more children. And I don't. She might go along with my wishes for a while. But I figure sooner or later she's going to start resenting me. I think—"

"You're thinking too damned much, Denver. Why don't you just let yourself enjoy the blessings you have right now instead of worrying about all the things that could go wrong?"

When Denver didn't answer, Rafe's eyes narrowed with speculation.

"What's wrong with having more children, anyway?" Rafe asked. "I realize kids are a big expense, but it's not like you're a pauper. You can afford to raise more than two kids. That is, maybe I'm getting ahead of myself. You'd have to really love Marcella before you'd want more children with her. And maybe you don't love her. At least, not yet."

Love her? Would that make everything all right? Would that take his fears away? Denver wondered. He'd loved Christa, but that hadn't kept her and the baby alive.

"You are getting ahead of yourself, Rafe. I'm...just now getting used to being with a woman again on a regular basis."

Rafe suddenly smiled and rose to his feet. "Yeah. I've been married for a few years now. I guess I expect you to feel about Marcella like I do Lilly. You couldn't live without her even if you wanted to."

Oh Lord, he did already feel that way about Marcella, Denver thought. So what did that mean? That he was already in love with her? He didn't want to think about it now. Like Rafe said, he needed to quit worrying and start enjoying.

"Okay, buddy," Rafe said, "let's go through this tack, and then I've got to head over to the office to make a few calls. Dad is thinking he wants another new herd to put on the far west range. I think I've located the kind of cattle he wants, but they're in Nebraska."

Glad for the change of subject, Denver stood. "He wants to buy them now? Just as we're heading into the dead of winter?"

Rafe chuckled. "Best time to save a dollar. And when it comes to cattle, he's like a kid at Christmas. And speaking of Christmas, don't tell the hands, but they're all getting new saddles this year."

Denver's jaw fell open. "Are you kidding me?"

"No. Santa Claus is going to deliver some heavy loads to the Silver Horn this Christmas."

"Mom, are we going to eat turkey when we get to Denver's house?"

Marcella momentarily took her eyes off the graveled road to glance in the rearview mirror at Peter. He and Harry were both dressed in their better jeans and button-up shirts. Harry's red curls were tamed as neatly as possible, while Peter's blond bangs had been carefully brushed to one side. Except for when they went to church services, she'd never seen them take this much pains with their appearance, and she realized the effort was all for Denver's sake.

Denver. Just the thought of him filled her with happy warmth. She'd never dreamed that any man could make her feel so desirable or special. Making love to him had taken her on a wondrous journey, and the miracle of their deep connection had seeped into every aspect of her life. Now everything from the sight of a gray winter sky to a grateful smile of a patient seemed to hold a special meaning for Marcella.

Yes, Denver had changed her life, she thought. And though she couldn't predict where their relationship was headed, she knew she could search far and wide and never find a better man for her and the boys.

"I don't know what we'll be eating, Peter," Marcella answered. "Does it really matter?"

"No. I just wondered. Can a man cook good things?"

Harry scoffed at his brother's question. "You see all those guys cooking on TV, don't you?"

"Yeah, but that doesn't mean the stuff they cook is good. Besides, I don't believe everything I see on TV."

"Now, that's being smart, Peter," Marcella spoke up. "Your brother needs to follow your example."

"Well, Mom, lots of chefs are men," Harry said defensively.

"True," Marcella reasoned. "But it's like Peter says. That doesn't necessarily mean that what they cook tastes good."

Peter scooted as far to the edge of his seat as the safety belt would allow. "Will Denver's Thanksgiving dinner taste good, Mom?"

She kept her smile to herself. "I hope so. But even if it tastes horrible, you guys are going to act like everything is delicious. Hear me? Denver has worked hard to make dinner for us and I want both of you boys to be polite and gracious."

"Gracious? What's that?" Peter asked.

"Well, it means nice."

"Aw, Mom, we aren't going to say anything bad to Denver," Harry insisted. "We love him. Don't we, Peter?"

"Yeah. He's super. He'd be the most awesome dad we could ever have. Right, Harry?"

"Right!"

Marcella glanced in the mirror just in time to see the two boys giving each other an exuberant high five. And for one split second she considered pulling the car over to the side of the road and reminding her sons that there were no plans being made for Denver to become their father. And for everyone's sake, they needed to get the idea out of their heads.

But she instantly nixed that idea. It was Thanksgiving. Why spoil their special day by crushing their childish dreams? Besides, she had her own dreams about Denver. And for today, at least, she wanted to believe they could come true.

A few minutes later, Marcella turned onto the long narrow drive that led up to Denver's house. This was the first time since the night of the Halloween party that she and the boys had visited his home. Now in the light of day, she could see the outside walls of the low, rambling ranch house were covered with light gray siding and native rock work that went halfway up. Slate colored shutters trimmed the windows, and a long covered porch sheltered the front entrance. A stand of pines grew tall in the small front yard, while the bare limbs of several poplars promised the house would be shaded by hot summertime.

"Wow! There's a mountain right behind Denver's house," Harry exclaimed. "Can me and Peter climb it?"

The slope was more like a tall hill than a mountain and sparsely dotted with trees and vegetation. Marcella realized the sight of all this open space was like dipping into a candy box for Harry and Peter. "Maybe later. After we've had our meal."

"Yay, Mom!" Peter yelled out, then poked a defiant face at Harry. "Bet I can beat you to the top!"

"Hah, I'll leave you in the dust, scrawny!"

Moments later, as the three of them stepped onto the porch, the boys were still debating who could make the climb faster, but when Denver opened the door, they instantly forgot about the challenge.

"Hi, Denver! Thank you for inviting us to dinner!"

The boys chimed out the greeting in perfect unison, which promptly put a grin on Denver's face.

"Thank you for coming," he told them as he pushed the door wide.

"Hello, Marcella." He winked at her as she stepped past him and into the house. "That's a good-looking pair of guys you brought with you."

"They'll do," Marcella said, her affectionate glance encompassing both her sons.

"We even took a shower this morning," Harry admitted as he and Peter followed the adults into the living room. "Just like we were going to school."

Denver chuckled. "I feel honored."

He helped Marcella out of her coat, then waited for

Peter and Harry to hand over theirs. Once Denver had hung the garments in a nearby closet, Peter lifted his nose to the air and sniffed. "Gee, something sure smells good! And I'm hungry."

"It'll be ready in about thirty minutes," he said. "Then you can tell me whether it tastes as good as it smells."

Harry immediately spoke up. "Mom says we have to tell you it's good even if it isn't."

Marcella gasped, then groaned with embarrassment. "Harry! Am I going to have to put a zipper on your mouth?"

Denver laughed loudly, then made a tsking noise at Marcella. "Are you teaching Peter and Harry to tell fibs?"

Deciding there was nothing else to do but laugh along with him, she said, "I'm trying to teach them to be polite, but obviously they haven't gotten the hang of it yet."

Denver wrapped an arm around each boy's back and urged them out of the living room. "Come on, guys. I have something in the kitchen I want to show you."

"Am I invited, too?" Marcella asked impishly.

He glanced at her and grinned, and the twinkle in his eyes was for her and her alone.

"Of course you're invited. I might need to put you to work."

The four of them marched through the house, which was much more spacious than Marcella's. As soon as they stepped into the kitchen, she stared around in wonder. Except for the pots on the stove and a few last-minute preparations scattered on the cabinet counter, everything looked clean and tidy. Even the tiled floor was sparkling.

"Looks like you've had a maid hard at work in here," Marcella teased. "I can actually see a kitchen now."

"Ha! These hands of mine have never worked so hard," Denver told her. "And that includes branding season."

He motioned for them to follow him over to the end of the cabinets, where he pointed to a big straw basket on the floor. "Harry and Peter suggested that I needed some cats. So I took their advice. What do you guys think?"

Marcella peeped around Denver's shoulder to see two sleeping kittens curled tightly together. One was solid white, the other gray. The sight of the baby animals took her by surprise. She hadn't imagined a rugged cowboy like him taking the time or effort to care for two fragile pets.

"Cats!" Harry quickly dropped to his knees and leaned over the basket. "Oooh, they're cool!"

Peter instantly sank to the floor next to his brother. "Look how little and pretty they are!"

"Their fur is really long," Harry said with awe. "I'll bet they could win a cat show!"

Chuckling, Denver glanced at Marcella, then down to her sons, who were getting as close to the kittens as they possibly could without actually touching them.

Denver said, "They're show cats, all right. Straight from the horse barn. The mother cat had four babies. Now that they're big enough to eat without her, I took two and Rafe's kids got the other two."

"What's their names?" Harry wanted to know.

"They don't have any yet," Denver told him. "I thought I'd let you guys name them for me. Since you two are responsible for me getting a pair of pets."

Peter reared his head back so that he could look up at Denver. "Gosh, that's an honor," he said, then looked over at Harry. "We better come up with something really good."

"Yeah, something better than Tom and Morris," Harry agreed.

"Maybe you better find out if they're girls or boys before you start thinking up names," Marcella suggested.

She'd hardly gotten the words out of her mouth when the kittens stirred and began to meow at their human admirers.

"The white one is a girl and the gray a boy," Denver told the boys, then wrapping a hand around Marcella's arm, he urged her to the other side of the room. "That will give them something to do until dinnertime."

"And what am I supposed to do?" she wanted to know.

He slanted her a seductive grin as he bent to open the oven door. "Stand here next to me and look pretty. That's more than enough to make me happy."

He pulled out a blue granite roaster, and Marcella's stomach growled as the smell of ham permeated the air around them.

"Seriously, Denver. Do I need to set the table? Or get the glasses ready?"

"Since today is a special day, we're eating in the dining room. And I've already set the table. See, I've been slaving in here for hours," he teased. "You're going to have to think of some special way to repay me for all this work."

Stepping closer, she said for his ears only, "Hmm. It'll take a lot of thinking, but I'll come up with something."

He set the roaster on top of the stove, then reached back into the oven for another similar baking pan. When he placed it alongside the one holding the ham, she grabbed a pot holder and curiously lifted the lid to see several Cornish hens browned to perfection.

"Oh my, you really have been slaving," she said. "Wait until I tell Paige about this. She's already jealous that my man is cooking for me today."

He paused to look at her, and Marcella was once again

struck by how handsome he looked today in faded blue jeans and a sexy black shirt with the sleeves rolled back against his forearms.

"Hey, I like the sound of that—'my man.' Want to say it again just to make me happy?"

She moved close enough to wrap her arm around his back. "My man," she repeated. "I like the sound of it, too."

"I think I remember you telling me that Paige is also a nurse. Does she have a family to celebrate today with?"

"Only an elderly grandfather. Which is just as well. She's pulling a double shift in the ER. And fixing dinner for the two of them later."

"Too bad injuries and illnesses don't take a holiday." He put down the pot holder and turned toward her. "I meant to tell you to invite your mother today, and then I forgot. She probably thinks I'm a heel."

Marcella could feel her face turning pink. "Don't worry about it," she said wryly. "She doesn't think you're suitable for me anyway."

Faint amusement crossed his face. "How could she make that determination? She hasn't met me yet."

"No. But you're bound to meet her sooner or later. So I should probably warn you right now that she doesn't like cowboys. In her mind, you all smell like manure and chewing tobacco."

Instead of being offended, he merely chuckled, and Marcella admired his easygoing manner. What short time she'd been married to Gordon, he'd railed about Saundra's opinionated personality.

"Sounds like she's not a bit judgmental," he joked.

Marcella gave him a lopsided grin. "She's always been very opinionated, to say the least. And she has this notion that her daughter needs a banker or doctor or someone like that to make her happy."

He shrugged good-naturedly. "Hmm. So she believes you need a professional guy with plenty of money. Well, she's your mother. She wants the best for you."

Marcella shook her head. "She doesn't know what's best for me. Anyway, Mom is working today. Tips are always better on holidays."

He said, "My parents are spending the day with my sister in Gillette. Frankly, I'm surprised they made the long drive."

"Oh? Do they not get away from the ranch very often?"

He pulled a lid off the back burner and gave the contents a stir. "No. When it comes to the livestock, my parents are both mother hens. They don't trust anyone to take care of things on the ranch like they would."

"Do you think your parents would like me and the boys?" she asked thoughtfully.

He hesitated, making Marcella wonder if the notion of introducing her to his parents made him feel uncomfortable. Perhaps they might frown upon their son getting involved with a woman who already had children. Or could be he was thinking Marcella was trying to rush their relationship into something far more serious than he wanted it to be. Whatever the reason, his pause left her feeling uncertain.

"My parents would be crazy about you. All three of you," he finally said. "Would you like to make a trip to Wyoming to meet them sometime?"

Even though his *sometime* probably meant far in the future, the unexpected invitation caused her nose-diving spirits to suddenly soar.

"I'd like that very much. I've never been to Wyoming.

And I already know I'd enjoy meeting your parents. They have to be nice people."

A skeptical grin slanted his lips. "And how could you know that?"

She let out a low, suggestive laugh. "Because you're so nice."

"Flatterer."

She started to give him a teasing retort when Harry and Peter trotted over to them.

"We've named the new kitties!" Peter declared.

"We thought about the names real hard, too. Want to hear 'em?" Harry asked.

"Sure we do. But first we need a drumroll for this announcement." Denver picked up a fork and spatula and drummed the utensils loudly against the top of one of the roasters. "And the names are—"

The youngsters exchanged comical glances, then giggled, and Marcella couldn't remember a time she'd seen her sons so happy.

"The girl's name is Star," Peter proudly announced. "'Cause she's white and pretty like a star in the sky."

"And the boy's name is Smokey," Harry added. "'Cause he's gray like smoke."

"Star and Smokey. I think those are two mighty fine names," Denver told them, then winked at Marcella. "That effort deserves double helpings of dessert, don't you think?"

Before agreeing to that idea, Peter wanted to know, "What is dessert gonna be?"

Marcella let out a good-natured groan and Denver laughed. "It's a secret," he told Peter. "You'll find out after we eat the main stuff. So you two go wash while your mother helps me put everything on the table."

The youngsters hurriedly left the kitchen to do his

bidding. When they'd disappeared from view, Marcella stepped over and slipped her arms around his rib cage.

With her head tilted back, she smiled up at him. "Thank you, Denver," she said softly. "For making this day so special for the boys. And me."

His fingertips traced a gentle circle on her cheek. "You're making my day pretty special, too," he told her. "Last year for Thanksgiving I ate a steak and watched football. Alone."

"There are plenty of guys who'd think that was the perfect day," she reasoned.

He shook his head. "Today with you and the boys— this is the way Thanksgiving Day should be."

Rising on her tiptoes, she pressed a swift kiss to his lips. Denver curled an arm around her waist and pulled her tight against him.

"Mmm. Don't tell Peter I got dessert early."

"Naughty boy," she said with a low chuckle, then eased out of his arms just as the two boys returned to the kitchen.

Much later after the huge meal was consumed, Marcella helped Denver deal with the leftovers while Peter and Harry went outside to explore the backyard.

She was snapping a lid on a container of candied sweet potatoes when her cell phone rang. Picking it up from where she'd placed it on a utility table, she immediately identified the caller as Lilly.

"Hello," Marcella answered cheerfully. "Happy Thanksgiving."

"Same to you," her friend replied. "Are you guys finished eating? Or are you going to have dinner later this evening?"

"We're just cleaning the kitchen," Marcella informed her, then looked over to Denver. "And I'm stuffed. I've learned a valuable lesson today. Cowboys can cook. Everything was delicious."

Lilly laughed. "Uh, you need to repeat that to Rafe. He can't open a can of soup. I'm glad to hear Denver fed you good. I didn't know he had it in him."

At that moment Denver glanced over at her, and Marcella gave him a sly smile. "He's full of surprises. So what's up with you?"

"Actually, I'm calling to see if the boys would like to go with us for a short visit with Clancy and Olivia. We're going to take the kids on a little hike down the mountain to look at the old mine."

Clancy and Olivia had a beautiful mountain home a few miles north of the main ranch house, but still on Silver Horn land. Marcella had visited the place once, when she and Lilly had gone to see their son, Shane, right after he was born. Marcella was certain Peter and Harry would enjoy the trek, but the word *mine* had her a little freaked. She'd seen several injuries come into the ER because people ventured into old deserted mines.

Frowning with uncertainty, she said, "An old mine sounds dangerous for kids to be around, Lilly."

"No worries, Marcella. The entrance is safely fenced off. There's no way any of the children can get too close. I promise we'll only be looking from afar, and Rafe and Clancy will be there to keep everyone corralled. I think the boys would really enjoy it. Clancy had the old flume reconstructed, so Harry and Peter can see how the ore used to be washed."

Feeling more assured about the outing, Marcella said, "Well, that sounds safe enough. And it would be a learning experience for them."

"Great," she interrupted. "We'll be by to pick them up in about fifteen minutes. See you then."

Lilly swiftly ended the call, and shaking her head, Marcella placed the phone back on the utility table.

"What was that about?" Denver asked.

With a smile of concession, she shrugged. "Rafe and Lilly are coming by to pick up the boys. They're taking the kids up to Clancy and Olivia's for a hike down the mountain to see some old mine. Do you think it's safe to let them go?"

Chuckling, he tossed the dish towel he was holding onto the counter and walked over to her. The glint in his eyes was full of promises as he gently cupped a hand around her chin. "I assure you it will be a very safe outing for Harry and Peter. But I can't guarantee your safety while they're gone."

Oh, she'd be more than physically safe with Denver, she thought. At times his touches were so tender just thinking of them brought a mist of tears to her eyes. No, when she was in Denver's hands, she was in the most sheltered place on earth. It was the safety of her heart that was in constant jeopardy while he was around.

Denver was rapidly changing her life and the whole outlook of her future. She'd never dreamed she would find a man who might care for her and her children. But now that he was welcoming them into his world, she didn't want to think of ever leaving it.

Rising up on her toes, she brought her lips next to his. "I'll take my chances."

Chapter Ten

An hour later, behind the locked door of Denver's bedroom, Marcella lay cuddled next to Denver's side, her head cushioned on his bare chest. The lightweight comforter he'd thrown over them after they'd made love cocooned them with cozy warmth, and as she listened to the slow, even rhythm of his heartbeat, she felt her eyelids getting heavy.

"Mmm. That was much better than pumpkin pie and whipped cream," he murmured huskily.

"Thanks," she teased. "I always did want to be compared to a piece of pie."

His calloused hand moved against the silky skin of her back, and Marcella closed her eyes and marveled at the warm contentment pouring through her. No man had ever made her feel so perfect and protected, or so wanted. And though she wasn't quite ready to admit it to herself, she feared she was falling in love. Not the hot crush kind of love that quickly burned itself out. But the deep sort of love that meant caring and giving for a lifetime.

What would Denver think, she wondered, if he guessed where her feelings were headed? He'd told her he was no longer in love with his late wife, and she wanted to believe that was true. But he'd also lost a child, and she wasn't at all sure he wanted to invest that much of his heart a second time. Would the time come when she'd have to choose between him and having more children?

A belated chuckle rumbled in his chest and thankfully the sound was enough to push the uneasy thoughts from her mind.

"That was a huge compliment, my dear," he said, then glanced over at the digital clock on the nightstand. "As much as I hate to, we'd better get up and get dressed before Lilly and Rafe return with the boys."

"Aw," she complained. "Lilly said they'd be gone at least two hours. We still have one more to go."

"That's right. But I thought we'd use that time to take a hike up the hill behind the house. I want you to see the view from up there."

Rising up on her elbow, she cast a provocative glance over his face and upper body. "The view I have right now looks mighty darn good to me."

Laughing lightly, he gently swatted her bare bottom. "Little vixen."

She squealed in playful protest and grabbed at the comforter as he tossed it aside.

"Too late," he told her, grinning. "Now you have to get dressed or freeze."

"I'll get you for this, Denver Yates," she muttered as she moved off the bed and snatched her clothing off the floor.

"I'm counting on it."

Ten minutes later, the two of them were walking side by side up the steep hill behind Denver's house. Sometime during the past hour, clouds had moved in to cover the afternoon sun and a brisk wind was quickly dropping the temperature.

Thankfully, Marcella had worn jeans and a sweater today just in case she might be outdoors. Now her coat and woolen scarf felt good against the winter weather.

"It looks like snow is coming," she commented as they paused next to a large boulder to catch their breath. "And not all of our last snowfall has melted yet."

"That's good," he said. "Come spring we'll have good grass."

Come spring. Would they still be together? she wondered. Would she still look at him and ache with longing? She didn't want to think about those questions today. She wanted to simply enjoy, but for some odd reason they kept popping into her mind.

Shaking away the deep thoughts, she looked at him and smiled. "Spoken like a true rancher. All you're worried about is green grass, fresh water and a herd of fat cows."

"And a beautiful woman next to my side. Don't forget that."

Snaking an arm around the back of her waist, he urged her forward. "Can you climb a bit higher? We're almost to the point I wanted you to see."

"I'm fine," she assured him. "Onward and upward."

They climbed a hundred or more yards on up the hill until they reached a small plateau facing northwest. Except for a few twisted junipers growing out of the shale-layered hillside, there was nothing to block the view, and as Marcella stood staring down at the sweeping plain that stretched far toward the western horizon, she couldn't help but gasp at the majestic sight.

"Oh my, this is breathtaking," she said. "Is all of this land a part of the Silver Horn?"

"As far as your eye can see. It stops just shy of the California state line."

"Incredible," she said with awe. "I can see the Sierra Mountain range from here!"

"That's right." He pointed to a spot where some type of evergreens made an emerald-colored ribbon across a wide stretch of valley floor. "Over there is Salt Cedar Flats. That winding band of trees marks the river. In the heat of summer, the flats will be full of mama cows and their calves. But for now we've moved them off that range so they'll be more protected from the weather."

The pride in his voice had her glancing up at him. "You really love this place, don't you?"

A smile of concession touched his lips. "I do love it."

"You say that like it's something you've never thought about before."

He shrugged. "When I first came here to the Horn, I only expected it to be a job. Just a means to provide for myself. I never dreamed or imagined it would become my life."

"So when you first came here, you had different plans for yourself?" she asked. "To work on this ranch for a while and move on? Or were you thinking you'd eventually get a place of your own?"

He nodded. "In the beginning that's exactly what I'd planned. To save my money until I could put a down payment on some property. But slowly and surely the Calhouns became my second family. The more I helped them work the land and the livestock, the more I fell in love with the place. Now it's impossible to picture myself ever leaving the Silver Horn."

"Even for a place of your own?"

His smile was full of conviction. "If I wanted to, I could get myself a herd of cattle and a string of horses. And Bart would allot me plenty enough acreage to support them. But I don't want that. I like being a part of something big. With all of us guys working together. No, I have everything I need or want right here."

Everything. Would there ever be room here for her and the boys? It was too soon to ask him that question. But someday in the not-too-distant future, she would have to ask it. Because as much as she was beginning to care for Denver, it would be pointless and heartbreaking to chase after an impossible dream.

He moved behind her and wrapped his arms around her waist and snuggled her close against him. The shelter of his hard body partially shielded her from the snow that had started to fall moments earlier.

Pressing his cheek against the side of her hair, he said, "Looks like we'd better start down. Before the weather gets worse."

Suddenly she didn't want to leave this wild, beautiful spot. At this moment it felt like they were in a fairy-tale world, where nothing could tear them apart. "Oh, Denver, it's so beautiful up here. Can't we stay for a few more minutes?"

His arms tightened around her. "Anything for you, darlin'. I just don't want you to get too cold."

Turning slightly, she pressed her cheek against his down-filled coat. "I won't be cold. Not as long as I'm with you."

A week and a half later, Denver had just ridden back into the ranch yard after a long day in the saddle and was leading his bay horse, Skipper, into the barn when Rafe trotted up to his side.

"Where have you been?" he asked anxiously. "I've been calling and sending you text messages all afternoon. I was about to send out a search party for you."

Frowning, Denver pulled the cell phone from his shirt

pocket and checked the notifications. "Nothing showing on the phone. I rode up on Rimrock Canyon. The signal must have been lost."

"You rode all the way out there? Alone?"

He shot Rafe a tired look. "I left a note on your desk."

"I've been too busy to look at my desk."

Denver shut the wide wooden door behind them. "Well, you of all people know I wouldn't go that far away from the ranch without another man with me. Not in this weather. Davey went with me. I wanted to make sure all of the cattle were out of the canyon before another snowstorm comes through."

He started down the wide alleyway of the barn with the horse in tow.

Keeping in step, Rafe asked, "Did you see any?"

"Probably fifty or more head, along with the Hereford bull."

"Hell," Rafe cursed. "That's not good."

"My same thoughts. I'll take a few cowboys out tomorrow morning and try to round them up. If we can get them over the Rimrock, then it won't be much problem to herd them over to the south range. At least they'll have shelter there."

Rafe nodded. "That's exactly what I was thinking. We should be able to get feed and hay to them there. I'll saddle up and go with you."

In front of the tack room, Denver wrapped the horse's reins around a hitching post and began to unbuckle the breast collar and cinch strap. While he worked, he could hear some of the guys at the other end of the barn singing "Jingle Bells."

When he looked over his shoulder at the cowboys, he could see they were nailing big red bows above each horse stall.

"Looks like the guys are starting to celebrate Christmas early," Denver commented.

Rafe chuckled. "You should know by now that Christmas starts early on the Silver Horn. Lilly and Ava already have the big house decked out with Christmas trees and all sorts of decorations."

"I'll bet little Colleen and Austin are already making a list for Santa. If I remember right, Austin asked for a pony last year. And he didn't get one. Is he still hoping Santa will come through on that request?"

Rafe laughed. "Austin was asking for a pony as soon as he got old enough to say the word. Now that he's three, I'm going to have to come through or I'm going to have a sad little boy on my hands."

An unexpected pang of loss suddenly shot through Denver. He didn't know how it would feel to watch the joy light up his own child's face on Christmas morning. And the hell of it, the thought of him reaching for such a gift was like staring off a dangerous cliff. He didn't think he'd ever be brave enough to make that leap into babies and family.

So how much longer are you going to lead Marcella on, Denver? She's beginning to think you're getting serious about her. Why don't you man up and confess that your feelings haven't changed? You're using her and the boys to fill a void. You have no intentions of making them your family. Ever.

"Denver? Did you hear me?"

Rafe's voice finally managed to push aside the accusing words sounding off in Denver's head, and he glanced over to see the ranch foreman frowning at him.

"Sorry, Rafe. I was thinking about something else. What were you saying?"

Rafe's eyes squinted skeptically as he looked at Denver.

"I was asking if you're planning to have Marcella and the boys out to your place for Christmas. Since Thanksgiving seemed to go over well for you."

Thanksgiving Day with Marcella and her boys had been one of the happiest days he'd spent in years. And for a while that day he'd let himself imagine how things might be if he did make them his family. But later that night, before Marcella and the boys had left to go home, he'd sat watching her curled up in front of the fireplace, the glow of the flames etching her lovely face, and uneasiness had crept in to spoil the joy he'd been feeling.

And all sorts of tragic scenarios had begun to roll through his head. What if she got pregnant? What if he lost her? How could he bear that much pain a second time? Since then, he'd been wondering if he was fooling himself that this happiness he had with Marcella could continue.

"Uh, we haven't decided yet where we'll celebrate Christmas. Maybe at my place again. The boys love it out here on the ranch."

Denver lifted the saddle from Skipper's back and carried it into the tack room. When he returned to the horse, Rafe had already gone to work brushing the mud off the animal's legs and tail.

"I'll do that," Denver told him, while reaching for the brush. "It's getting late. I'm sure Lilly's probably waiting to have supper."

Rafe handed him the brush. "Yeah, I'm about to head that way. I just wanted to let you know Dad located some hay. The semi should arrive tomorrow afternoon."

"That's good news."

"Damn right. I was getting worried about the hay situation, but that's taken care of. So we need to make sure there are a few barn hands around to unload it.

Otherwise, we'll need our best wranglers to help with rounding those cattle out of the canyon."

"It won't be easy."

He started to leave, then, appearing to have a second thought, paused. "Are you all right?"

Denver glanced in Rafe's direction. "Yeah. Sure. Why, do I look sick or something?"

His eyes squinting, Rafe shook his head. "No. You just seem a little preoccupied, that's all."

Preoccupied was hardly the word for it, Denver decided. Ever since Thanksgiving, his mind had been swimming in thoughts of Marcella. The more he dwelled on her, the more he felt like he was drowning. "I'm just thinking about tomorrow and the work we have ahead of us."

Nodding, Rafe gave his shoulder an encouraging slap. "All in stride, good buddy. See you in the morning."

"Sure. I'll be here in the barn saddling up first thing," Denver told him.

Later that night in the ER, Marcella and Paige had just finished attending to a man who had supposedly fallen on a sidewalk. However, the deep split in his lip coupled with a set of bruised knuckles made it clear to both nurses he'd been in some sort of altercation.

As the two of them stepped out of the sheeted cubicle, Paige said in a hushed voice, "I wonder what the other guy looks like?"

Marcella shook her head. "Probably worse. It's ridiculous how grown men can behave like children."

Paige's grunt was full of sarcasm. "It's in their jeans. That's *jeans* with a *J*."

Marcella was chuckling when her head suddenly

began to spin. Swaying in her tracks, she pressed a palm against her forehead. "Oooh! I'm...dizzy."

Quickly, Paige grabbed her arm to steady her. "Marcella! What's wrong?"

"I...I don't know." Her voice was dazed, her face white. "It came over me all of a sudden—I feel light-headed."

"Come on," Paige said firmly, slipping her arm around Marcella's back and gently urging her toward an empty treatment cubicle. "I'm going to get Dr. Sherman."

"Don't be silly," she protested. "The swimmy feeling is already going away."

Paige helped her take a seat on the end of an examining table. "You're not moving until we find out why you got the swimmy feeling in the first place."

Marcella wiped a shaky hand across her brow and was surprised to find it damp and clammy. "I just need a snack, that's all. I'm running on empty."

"Stay where you are," Paige ordered, then hurried off to fetch the doctor.

Nearly two hours later, Marcella was in the nurses' locker room, gathering her things to go home, when Paige strode up and opened the adjoining locker.

"Feeling better?" She pulled a tote bag from the storage space and glanced over at Marcella. "At least you have a bit of rose on your cheeks now. For a while there you looked ghastly."

Sighing, Marcella turned and sat down on a long wooden bench. As she pulled the pens from her coiled hair and shook it free, she tried to center her thoughts, but they were as scattered as a flock of frightened birds flying in all directions.

After a somewhat lengthy examination by Dr. Sherman, he'd sent a sample of her blood to the lab for a quick pregnancy test. No one had been more stunned than Marcella when the results had returned positive.

She was going to have a baby. Denver's baby!

"Paige, I don't know whether to shout with joy or burst into tears. I...I'm still in shock."

Paige sank onto the bench and reached for Marcella's hand. Giving it a comforting pat, she said, "Oh, honey, everything will be all right. You've wanted another baby for so long. And you never thought it would happen. Your dream is coming true. So celebrate. That's what I say."

Marcella squeezed her eyes tight as emotional tears threatened to spill over onto her cheeks. "I am happy. But my feelings about the situation hardly matter. I have Denver and the boys to consider."

Paige shook her head. "I can't count the times you've told me that Peter and Harry have begged you for a brother or sister."

Marcella choked back a helpless groan. "Yes, but when my sons think of getting a sibling, it's in the context of a real family...with a daddy in the house. This is—well, I'm still a single mother. And Denver is..."

When her words trailed off, Paige asked sagely, "Not ready to be a father? Then all I can say is it's time he get ready."

Still stunned by Dr. Sherman's diagnosis, she stared at her friend. "I don't know how this happened, Paige! I haven't missed a pill. I haven't missed a period. Granted, the last one was very light, but that's not unusual for me. I had a bit of a cold virus a few weeks ago. Dr. Sherman said that might have had some effect on my birth control. Or he says it's possible that I just happened to fall into the tiny percent that fails for some unknown reason. Paige, before I met Denver, I didn't need birth control pills! I only took them to keep me regular. Sex wasn't exactly on my grocery list!"

Paige gave her hand another reassuring pat. "It doesn't matter how it happened. That's already water under the bridge. Now the main thing is for you to be happy and healthy. And frankly, I couldn't be happier for you. If anyone deserves another baby, it's you, little mother." Leaning over, she pecked a kiss on Marcella's cheek. "Congratulations. I'll see you tomorrow. Go home and get some rest."

"Yes, good night, Paige," she murmured dazedly.

Tomorrow. The word continued to linger in Marcella's mind as she rose to her feet and gathered up her tote and handbag. What was she going to do about telling Denver? She'd promised him her birth control was safe. But as Dr. Sherman had just reminded her, abstinence was the only thing that was a hundred percent foolproof. The baby growing inside her was certainly confirmation of that. Now all she could hope for was that Denver would understand and be happy about their unexpected miracle.

It took Denver and Rafe, plus six more wranglers, working two whole days to finally round up the last of the cattle in the canyon and herd them over the Rimrock. And just in time, too, as another snowstorm was predicted to drop at least four or five fresh inches in the next few days.

Denver couldn't remember a winter being this wet, and though he and the Calhouns welcomed the life-giving moisture, he had to admit he was getting weary of the gray skies. Or maybe it was the time away from Marcella that was putting him in a bit of a melancholy mood. Whatever the reason, he was glad he had enough of a break in his schedule this morning to drive into town and see her before she went to work.

The moment she opened the door and he stepped over the threshold, he scooped her up in his arms and wrapped his lips over hers. The taste of her kiss was like a drink of water after a long thirst.

"Denver!" she squealed, once he finally lifted his head. "The door is still open!"

"So it is, my beautiful redhead." Turning, he pushed the door shut with the toe of his boot, then with her legs dangling over his arm, he managed to reach the doorknob and twist the lock. "Now I have you all to myself and I can't wait to make love to you."

"Denver! I haven't seen you in days! We need to talk first!"

He carried her through the living room and turned into the short hallway that led to the bedroom. "We'll have plenty of time to talk later," he said, his voice gruff with desire. "I've been aching these past days and you're the only nurse who can cure me."

With a smile of surrender, she wrapped her arms tightly around his neck and pressed her lips to his cheek. "I guess the talking can wait until I cure this ache of yours."

In the dim confines of her bedroom, Denver wasted no time stripping off her jeans and sweater. After she was naked and lying in the middle of the bed, he hurriedly got undressed to join her.

The moment he stretched out beside her, she rolled into his arms. Denver's chest swelled with emotions as he gathered her tight against him and kissed her giving mouth. He didn't know how it had happened, but in a short matter of weeks, she'd become his whole world. Now he couldn't imagine his life without her.

"Oh, I've missed you," he said against her lips. "Every hour, every minute, I'm away from you is too long."

Her soft hands glided over the tops of his shoulders and up the sides of his neck until they were cupping his jaw. When Denver looked at her face, he was struck by the glaze of moisture in her blue eyes.

"Marcella," he whispered gently. "Is something wrong?"

Even though her warm lips tilted into a smile, a tear oozed from the corner of one eye.

"No. It's just that...I feel the same way. I want you near me. Always."

With the pad of his forefinger, he wiped the moisture away from her eye. And in that instant, he'd never felt closer to anyone in his life. The deep connection filled him up until he thought his heart would burst from it.

"My sweet, sweet Marcella." His throat was so tight her name came out as a husky whisper, and then it was impossible to say another word as she lifted her head from the pillow and planted her lips over his. That was all it took to shut down his thinking and allow his body to take over.

For the next several minutes all he knew was Marcella's warm body giving him everything he needed. Her kisses said she wanted him desperately, while her clinging hands declared she never wanted to let him go. And though he wanted to keep the end at bay, the sweet magic of her body was too potent. All too soon he was clutching her hips tight against his, gasping her name as he spilled his seed inside her.

When Denver finally moved off her, Marcella quickly rolled onto her side and blinked at the wall of tears blurring her eyes. She didn't know why this morning, of all mornings, their lovemaking had shaken her to the very depths of her being. The earth had done more than move for her. She'd left the planet completely and she still wasn't sure she was back to safety.

Was it the baby making her extra emotional? Or was it the desperate fear clawing inside her that was making her feel unworldly and vulnerable?

The warmth of his hand settled over her hip, and she closed her eyes and tried to swallow away the thickness in her throat.

"Are you okay?" he asked gently.

She turned to face him and did her best to smile. "I'm fine."

His fingertips traced a path over her cheekbone, to the corner of her mouth, then on to the middle of her chin. The gentle touch was as mesmerizing as the glow in his brown eyes.

"I'm not sure. You seem a bit teary for some reason. Have I done something to upset you?"

She slipped her arm around him and pulled herself closer to the solid strength of his body. "Of course not. I'm just happy to finally see you again."

"Hmm." He pressed a kiss against her forehead. "I wanted to come sooner, but this damn weather is causing havoc on the ranch. For the past two days we've been rounding up cattle and moving them out of the canyon."

"Oh. That's not a good place for them in the winter?"

"When it snows this much, it gets too deep for them to walk, much less find anything to eat. And the only access we have into the canyon is by horseback, so we can't haul hay and feed to them."

"I see. So do you have the cattle settled where you need them now?"

"Finally. So I mentioned to Rafe that I wanted to make

a quick trip into town to see you this morning. He practically pushed me out of the barn." His grin was sly. "I think he and Lilly like the idea of us being together."

Yes, Lilly and Rafe had done some matchmaking, Marcella thought. What were those two going to think when they heard what their matchmaking had produced?

Forget about Lilly and Rafe's reaction. It's Denver's response that you need to be thinking about. So just tell him and get it over with. He'll either be happy or he won't. Either way it's time you dealt with it.

Shutting out the taunting voice in her head, she said, "I'm glad he could spare you. I've been wanting to talk with you and it's not something I wanted to get into over the phone."

"I've been wanting to talk with you, too," he said. "The Silver Horn is already getting decked out for Christmas and I've been thinking about Harry and Peter. They told me you always decorate with a Christmas tree. Is that right?"

"Yes. I usually have one up by now. But things have been...a little hectic here lately."

"I'm glad you haven't gotten around to doing a tree yet. I wanted to see if you and the boys would like to come out to the ranch this weekend and we'll walk up the mountain behind the house. The boys can pick out the perfect tree and I'll cut it down and haul it here to the house for you. Or we can put it up in my house. It doesn't matter to me. As long as the four of us are together."

Her heart was suddenly bursting with emotion, and though the words *I love you* were on the tip of her tongue, begging to be released, she bit them back and drew in a long, bracing breath.

"It sounds wonderful, Denver. Yes, the four of us together. That's what I want, too. And the boys will be jumping up and down with excitement when I tell them."

"Great. Then I'll supply the tree if you can come up with the decorations."

"I have plenty of those stored away," she assured him. "And whether we put it here or in your house, we'll make it the most beautiful tree ever."

He kissed her forehead again, then pulled his head back far enough to look at her. "Okay, we have that settled. So what did you want to talk to me about? Are the boys okay? Peter's asthma hasn't been acting up, has it?"

"No, the boys are good. And Peter's latest checkup with the doctor was an A-plus. It's not about them—exactly," she said, then glanced blindly down at the blanket covering their naked bodies. Telling him she was going to have his baby shouldn't be this hard, Marcella thought. This should be a happy, joyous announcement. Instead, uncertainty was chilling her to the point that she was close to shivering.

"Then what is it about?" he asked, his voice suddenly growing cautious. "Has something happened at the hospital? Something about your work?"

"No. I mean, something did happen—to me—at the hospital. Last night, to be exact. I had a dizzy spell and Dr. Sherman ended up giving me an examination and sending a sample of my blood to the lab."

Suddenly he was pressing her back against the mattress and his face was hovering over hers. Stark fear was in his eyes, and Marcella realized he was probably thinking back to his late wife's health problems.

"What's wrong?" he demanded. "Are you trying to tell me you have some sort of blood disease? Is that what those tears were about earlier?"

Her head twisted back and forth upon the pillow. "No.

I don't have any sort of disease. I'm…going to have a baby."

A stunned look washed over his face, and then he fell limply onto his back to stare silently up at the ceiling.

Marcella watched him for a moment, and then as the disappointment in her heart became too heavy to bear, she threw back the covers and reached for her clothes.

Chapter Eleven

"**W**here are you going?"

Marcella had just finished dressing and was starting out of the bedroom when Denver finally spoke. She turned back to him, her blood simmering with anger and pain.

"To the kitchen. I haven't had breakfast yet."

He rose up to a sitting position and stared at her in stunned fascination, which only made Marcella even angrier. Up until five minutes ago, she would have sworn he was a caring, sensitive man. But that description had gone up in smoke the moment she'd said the word *baby*.

"You mean you can think about eating at a time like this?"

"I can not only think about it. I can do it," she said bluntly, then walked out of the bedroom before he could add anything else.

She was in the kitchen brewing coffee and whisking eggs when he finally entered the room. Fully dressed, he tossed his hat onto the table and pulled out a chair.

As he sat down, Marcella tried to ignore the iron set of his jaw. "Would you like some eggs and toast?" she asked politely.

"No. I'd like to know what happened."

Resisting the urge to slam the whisk onto the cabinet counter, she placed it on a paper towel and walked over to him.

"Since you want to be crass and rude about this, I can be, too. So you're a big boy. You know what happened. We had sex. A baby was conceived."

His brows shot up. "And whose fault was that?" he demanded. "You assured me your birth control was safe. I trusted you!"

"I believed my birth control was adequate. But things happen. If you think I'm going to apologize for this baby, you're cracked in the head. As far as I'm concerned, it's a little miracle. As for you—well, you're a big disappointment, that's all."

He was suddenly sneering, and Marcella felt as though she was looking at a stranger instead of the man she loved.

"Things happen," he repeated mockingly. "Like tossing a pill into the trash instead of your mouth?"

Marcella had to literally clench her hands together to keep from slapping him. Dear God, she was a nurse who'd spent years soothing wounds. But at this very moment she actually wanted to inflict physical pain on another human being. The realization was proof of just how low he'd caused her emotions to sink.

"You honestly think I would do something that deceitful?" she asked, her voice vibrating with anger and disbelief.

"I've already had one woman do it to me. Why not you, too? You've already admitted how much you wanted more babies."

"Yes! With the right man. And I'm beginning to see that you're far from being the right one!"

In spite of her effort to control it, her voice was rising with each word. Blood was pounding inside her head, roaring in her ears. Never had she felt this furious at anyone or anything.

The accusing tone in his voice continued. "It's rather late to be drawing that opinion of me now, don't you think?"

"Late? Looks to me like I saw the real you just in the nick of time."

He let out a frustrated sigh. "Look, Marcella, I explained everything to you about Christa. From the very beginning you knew I didn't want anything to do with pregnancy or babies."

"That's right. But I was foolish enough to let you crawl into my bed anyway." She shoved a wave of tangled red hair off her face and stared at him, her eyes blazing. "Because I had the stupid idea you might begin to care for me. Really care. That you would change your mind about babies and having a family."

When he failed to make a response, she let out a harsh laugh and marched back over to the cabinet. Picking up the whisk, she gave the eggs another vicious stir.

"Don't worry, Denver. You're off the hook. Actually, now that I think of it, you never were on the hook. Because deep down I had the feeling you were going to react like this." The look she shot him was sharp enough to bore through granite. "I've been a single mother of two sons for a long time. It doesn't scare me to be a single mother of three children. And as far as I'm concerned, I'll be the happiest woman alive if I never see your face again. So get the hell out of my house!"

His hard expression swiftly turned to one of utter disbelief. "Is that how you really feel?"

Feel? She wanted to scream at him. How did he expect

her to feel anything? In the past few minutes he'd stomped her emotions into nothing more than a quivering heap.

Turning her back to him, she said numbly, "It's exactly how I feel."

He said nothing, and a few seconds later she heard the scrape of his chair and then his footsteps leaving the kitchen. When the sound of the front door opening and closing finally reached her, she allowed herself to breathe again. And her tears to fall.

The following week passed in a weary daze for Marcella. At work she did her best to focus on her job. Tending the needy patients who entered the ER helped to keep her mind off Denver. At least the sick and injured needed and appreciated her care. That was more than she could say about him.

What do you expect, Marcella? Denver never told you he loved you. You were expecting things from him that were never going to happen. His talk about missing you and spending Christmas with you was nothing more than sweet talk. Nothing more than a man saying the right things just to give his sex partner enough hope to keep her hanging on.

The bitter voice going on in Marcella's head very nearly drowned out Paige's as the two women sat at a table in the hospital cafeteria.

"Marcella, you're not eating. Are you nauseated?"

She glanced down at the bowl of stew on her tray. "No. I'm okay."

"If you're so okay, why aren't you eating? You of all people know how important nutrition is for the first few weeks of an embryo's life. So eat up and feed the little guy!" she ordered.

Smiling wanly, Marcella straightened her slumped

shoulders and dipped into the stew. "How do you know the baby is a boy?"

"All right, so feed the little girl and quit mooning over that cowboy. Why would you even want a man who left you as soon as you told him you were pregnant? He's obviously a first-class jerk!"

"He didn't leave, Paige," Marcella corrected her friend. "I ordered him out of the house and out of my life."

"Doesn't matter," she said between bites of a tuna fish sandwich. "Either way, he's gone. No flowers or words of comfort. No promises to be there for you and the little one. Creep. You need to mark a big X on his face and move on."

Even though Paige was right, it was impossible to push Denver out of her heart and go on with her life. His baby was growing inside her. And she had no idea what that might mean for her and the baby's future. In spite of the asinine way he'd reacted to the news of her pregnancy, she had no doubt he was a responsible man. Otherwise, the Calhouns would've never gathered him to the bosom of their family and kept him there for twelve long years. Knowing that, she feared that sooner or later he might demand his fatherly rights to the child. And then what? It would be unbearably painful to share a child with a man who didn't love her.

"Paige, it's not that simple. Denver is the father. I can't block him out of the baby's life. Not if he decides he wants to be a father. It wouldn't be fair to him or the child."

Paige's lips pursed with disgust. "You're far nicer than I could ever be. I wouldn't give my ex the time of day. Much less anything else."

"It's easy for you to say that, Paige. You don't have children to consider."

"Thank God Larry and I didn't have kids," she muttered, then in a gentler tone asked, "Have you told Harry and Peter about the baby yet?"

Shaking her head, Marcella put down her spoon. "No. I need to take a little time to decide how best to explain everything. As much as a mother can explain to boys ten and eleven years old. The boys understand there are families without a daddy in the house. That's the only kind of life the three of us have had. But nothing about it is going to be easy." She let out a long breath and rubbed her fingertips against her burning eyelids. "Telling them at Christmas might be best. I can present the news to them as a gift."

Her expression tender, Paige reached over and squeezed Marcella's fingers. "The baby is a gift. No matter about Denver. Just focus on that."

"Believe me, Paige, that's the one thing that's holding me together." She picked up her spoon and tried to renew her interest in the stew. "Last night I sat Harry and Peter down and tried to explain about Denver and why he won't be in our lives anymore."

"Oh my. You've told me how close they've grown to Denver. That must've been rough."

Marcella's throat closed around the lump of potato she'd tried to swallow. She'd never seen her children more hurt and crestfallen. And it was her fault. All her fault for reaching for a love that could never be.

"It was one of the hardest things I've ever had to do. Peter started crying—you know how sensitive he is. Harry thinks he has to be the strong brother because he's older. So he set his jaw and went quiet. Too quiet." Sighing heavily, she leaned back in the plastic chair. "I hate that I've done this to them, Paige. And even worse, with Christmas coming. I want the boys to have a happy holiday."

"Aww, Peter and Harry will have a happy Christmas. They'll be thrilled about getting a new brother or sister. And as the days pass they'll hopefully start forgetting about Denver."

Marcella gave her a weary smile. "You're an optimist, my dear friend."

"Right. I'm optimistic that you'll soon find a real man who will appreciate you and treat you with love and respect. And I happen to know the perfect one," she added slyly. "He has an office upstairs."

Seeing where her friend's well-meaning advice was headed, Marcella groaned and shoved away the tray. "Please don't start in about Dr. Whitehorse again. Yes, he's nice. Yes, he's good-looking. But at this point I don't think I'll ever want another man in my life. Anyway, I'm pregnant."

Paige chewed the last bite of her sandwich, then shot her a knowing smile. "If a man really loved you, that would hardly stop him."

Yes, Marcella thought dourly, that was the whole problem. If Denver had really loved her, he would have been thrilled when she told him about the baby. He would've taken her in his arms and talked about their future together and vowed to always cherish and protect them. Instead, she'd gotten cold stares and angry accusations. The reality still sliced her with heavy pain.

Marcella reached for her handbag. "If you're finished, we need to be getting back. Helen is probably watching the clock."

Paige gathered the remnants of her meal and piled them on a tray. "You haven't noticed? Esther is filling in for Helen tonight. Helen has gone over to California for the weekend to celebrate an early Christmas with her son."

Helen, the iron lady, had been head nurse at Tahoe General ER for more years than Marcella could count. On her best days the woman was approachable; otherwise, she was a taskmaster. Yet all the nurses loved her. Because everyone could see that beneath her outward armor, she was as soft as a down pillow and somehow just as comforting. Marcella was certain that when Helen learned of her pregnancy, the veteran nurse would be the first to offer an encouraging word or helping hand.

"Well, I'm glad someone is having fun," Marcella said. "When does ours start?"

The two women rose to their feet, and with a little laugh, Paige curled an arm around the back of Marcella's waist. "It starts with our very next patient."

Later that evening on the Silver Horn, Denver stood in the office he shared with Rafe and stared out the dusty window at the twilight settling over the ranch yard. Except for a few cowboys checking water troughs and spreading hay in the holding pens, most of the men had quit for the day. To the far right, he could see smoke spiraling from the chimney in the bunkhouse. Inside the big log structure, the men would be shedding their heavy outerwear and hanging up their spurs and chaps. James, the bunkhouse cook, would be getting ready to dish up a hearty meal. Something with meat and potatoes and a rich dessert. Down the long pine table there would be plenty of conversation with jokes and laughter.

In many ways, Denver envied those men. None of them had to go home to an empty house or stare at the shadows on the wall and wonder how things might've been. Those men had chosen to be free of worries over a woman, or kids, or holding a family together. Yet he doubted most of them had ever experienced the incredible joy Marcella had given him for a few short weeks.

That morning after she'd told him she was pregnant, Denver had somehow gotten back to the ranch in one piece. But he didn't remember leaving her house, driving the thirty-five miles or anything else that might have happened in between. Shock must have caused him to have some sort of mental blackout. At least, he'd put the lack of consciousness down to that reason. Several days had passed before the haze had finally worn off enough for him to recall what the two of them had actually said to each other.

If I never see your face again, I'll be a happy woman.

Marcella's words continued to haunt him, and whether he died tomorrow or fifty years from now, he'd still remember the icy fury on her face when she'd said them.

What do you expect, Denver? You behaved like a complete swine. You never once thought about Marcella or her feelings. All you were concerned about was yourself and how you'd been wronged. You don't deserve a woman like her. And you certainly don't deserve a baby. So it's just as well she sent you packing.

The sound of the door opening and closing had Denver turning away from the window to see Rafe entering the office. A black woolen muffler was tied around his neck to block out any cold that might escape past the neck of his brown canvas coat. His face was pinched and red from the cold wind, but there was a cheery smile on his face. The sight of it grated on Denver's raw nerves. Why did his best buddy in the world get to be so happy, while Denver was so downright miserable?

"Oh, you're still here." Rafe walked over to a large space heater positioned a few feet away from the desks.

After removing his gloves, he thrust his hands toward the heat. "I was about to call you."

Doing his best to shake away his heavy thoughts, Denver left his spot at the window and walked over to where Rafe stood close to the heater.

"What's up?" he asked. "Anything wrong?"

Rafe glanced at him. "No. I came by to make sure everything here in the office was shut down. Instead, I find you."

Denver shrugged one shoulder. "I've been going over the feed orders. That's all."

Rafe's wry expression said he didn't believe a word Denver was saying. "Oh. You do that standing at the window? Staring off into space?"

Denver's nostrils flared. He wasn't ready to deal with Rafe's personal chitchat. And he sure wasn't ready to make some sort of revelation about his split with Marcella. It was still too raw and painful. "Is it a crime to look out the window? Or maybe you think I ought to be over there wiping it clean?"

Rafe merely looked at him and shook his head. "I thought it was too cold for any bees to be flying around, but apparently one found its way under your collar."

Grunting, Denver moved over to his desk and switched off the computer. "I'm not in the mood for your sarcasm."

"Well, frankly, I'm not too happy with you right now."

Denver squinted a questioning look at him. "Why? What have I messed up?"

"My wife," Rafe said. "Lilly is very unhappy because Marcella refuses to come out to a little party we're giving for Dad tomorrow night. Apparently, she doesn't want to get within ten miles of you."

Denver could feel his face turning red-hot. "I can't

help it if Marcella is being unsociable. We're not a couple anymore."

"Hmmp. Like Lilly and I haven't already figured that out for ourselves. Well, sometimes good intentions just don't work out. We thought you two would be the perfect pair—but life goes on."

Denver crossed the room and pulled his coat off a rack on the wall. As he put on the garment, he tried to ignore the heavy pain in his chest, but the weight of it was practically smothering him.

"Yeah, life goes on," he said tightly.

"So what about you?" Rafe asked. "Can we expect to see you tomorrow night? It's mostly going to be family and a few friends. Dad has asked Noreen to marry him and she's accepted. So it's just a little gathering for drinks and snacks and congratulations. I'm sure later on we'll be giving them a proper engagement party. But it's too close to Christmas for that. Especially with the barn party coming up this weekend."

Without looking Rafe's way, Denver zipped up his coat and jammed his hands into a pair of leather work gloves. Parties and gifts, holiday festivities, and now a wedding engagement. A week ago Denver had been making plans to have a special Christmas with Marcella and Harry and Peter. For the first time since Christa had died he'd felt as though he'd be celebrating yuletide with a family of his own. Now all those plans had been ripped to shreds.

"I'm not going to make any promises, but I'll try. I'm glad for Orin and Noreen. And I want him to know I wish them the best."

"Thanks, Denver. I realize you're not in a celebratory mood, but Dad considers you his son, too. It would mean a lot to him if you made an appearance. Even a brief one."

Denver slanted him a wary glance. "Are you sure Marcella won't be there?"

Rafe frowned. "I'm positive. Why? Something really bad must have happened between you two if you don't even want to be in the same room with her. Nor she with you."

Clearly Marcella hadn't shared the news about the coming baby with Lilly or Ava, Denver concluded. Otherwise, Rafe would have already heard about it and their subsequent breakup. Well, Denver was hardly in the mood to make the announcement, either. He was still trying to come to terms with the idea that he was going to be a father. Much less be comfortable discussing the matter with anyone.

For years after Christa and the baby had died, he'd sworn he'd never get another woman pregnant. He'd never wanted to risk putting his heart into another position where he stood to lose so much. But somehow it had happened. Now he was afraid to let himself think past tomorrow.

"I'm sorry, Rafe. I can't talk about it. Not now. I'm going home and fixing myself some supper."

He moved to the door and Rafe followed.

"Denver," he said soberly, "I'm sorry this had to happen. Lilly and I never meant for you or Marcella to get hurt. We thought—well, getting you two together would be a good thing. Apparently, we were wrong to play matchmakers and we both feel horrible about it."

Shaking his head, Denver said, "You two didn't do this to me. I did it to myself. So don't even think about taking the blame."

Slapping a hand on his shoulder, Rafe gave him a lopsided smile. "Okay. Let's forget it."

Forget it? As Denver stepped out into the cold night,

he realized he'd never be able to forget Marcella or put their broken affair behind him. A baby was coming. And no matter what happened between him and Marcella in the future, he wanted to be a part of his child's life.

But what if something goes wrong before the baby is ever born, Denver? What if you lose this child like the last one? What if something happens to Marcella, too? It will be your fault. Instead of blaming her, you need to be owning up to the fact that you got her pregnant.

The accusing voice in his head stayed with him through the short drive home. By the time he changed out of his dirty work clothes and walked into the kitchen, he was totally out of the mood for food. Which was just as well, as two hungry kittens raced over to him and quickly tried to climb the legs of his jeans.

"Whoa, you two! You don't have to tell me it's time for supper. I'll get it."

Realizing Smokey and Star needed human attention as much as they needed food nourishment, he took a few minutes to cuddle them before he doled canned food onto a clean saucer and placed it on the floor. While he sat at the table watching the duo go after the fishy meal with hungry gusto, he instinctively thought back to the day Peter and Harry had named the two kittens.

That Thanksgiving Day, Marcella's boys had been happy to be here in his home and excited to explore the vast outdoors of the ranch. The trip they'd taken with the Calhoun clan to see the old mine had been like a great adventure to them. When they'd returned, both boys had talked nonstop to him and their mother about all they'd seen and learned.

As Denver had listened to their happy chatter, he'd begun to imagine himself in the role of their father. He'd even allowed himself to think about the future and all the things he wanted to share with the boys. How much he wanted to guide and teach them.

All of that was gone now. He'd never be a father to Harry and Peter. At the most, he'd only get to be a part-time father to his own child.

Oh God, that wasn't the way he wanted things to be. But even if he could somehow rake up enough courage to deal with the pregnancy, he doubted she would ever forgive him. Maybe if she loved him, he might have a chance of making things right. But she'd never so much as hinted the word to him. And even if she had been harboring the feelings in her heart, he'd probably cut all those to pieces with his stupid, selfish behavior.

With a sigh of regret, he leaned over and stroked his fingers over the backs of both kittens. Harry and Peter probably hated him now, he thought. And the reality of losing the two boys hurt Denver almost as much as losing their mother.

Chapter Twelve

The next evening, on her way home from work, Marcella picked up a blue spruce from one of the many Christmas tree vendors that had sprung up around town for the approaching holiday. After a light dinner, her mother, Saundra, came over to help her erect the tree and join in on the trimming.

Normally, Harry and Peter were more than eager to hang bulbs and ornaments, but this year their effort was halfhearted, which only made Marcella feel worse.

"The boys act like one of the cats has died," Saundra said after the two boys had gone to their room to get ready for bed. "Or they've lost their best friend."

Marcella glanced over at her mother, who was pouring the last of the coffee into her cup. A few days ago, she'd revealed the news to her mother that she was expecting Denver's child. For the most part, Saundra had been supportive and sympathetic, yet she hadn't refrained from jabbing Marcella with an I-told-you-so now and then.

Marcella sank wearily into a kitchen chair. "They have lost their best friend, Mother. Denver had come to mean the world to them. They had big dreams that he would become their father. A real father. Now they've been let down again. I can only hope that this doesn't damage their ideals about manhood and what it means to grow up to be a responsible father. God knows they haven't had a good example to go by."

Shaking her head with disgust, her mother sank into the chair across from Marcella's.

"I tried to tell you about the man, honey, but you wouldn't listen. No, you thought Denver Yates was the grandest thing to come along since sliced bread. Now if—"

"I don't want to hear it, Mother," Marcella interrupted before Saundra could get rolling. "The last thing I need from you right now is a lecture."

Her lips pursed with disapproval, Saundra drummed her fingertips on the tabletop. "I'm not going to give you a lecture. But I am wondering about your plans. Have you told your father yet?"

Marcella blinked her eyes as tears burned at the backs of them. Since her father, Norval, had moved to California, she rarely had the chance to visit with him. A comforting hug from him right now would certainly be welcome.

"No. I plan to call him to wish him Merry Christmas. But I'm not going to tell him about the baby. Not yet."

Saundra frowned at her. "But why? Your father has always loved you. He won't be judgmental. He'll be excited to hear he's getting another grandchild. God knows, your brother, Spence, hasn't given us any."

"Spence is hardly ready to have children. He's still trying to get over his divorce. And frankly, I'm glad he's busy helping Grandma and Grandpa on the farm rather than chasing after another heartache," Marcella muttered.

Her mother clucked her tongue with disapproval. "You sound so jaded. You need to be thinking positive,

Marcella. Maybe this isn't the most ideal situation for a woman to be in, but I don't know anyone stronger than you are, my darling daughter. With or without a man, you'll make a nice life for your family."

Marcella smiled at her. "Thanks, Mother. Hearing you say that does make me feel better."

Smiling back at her, Saundra said, "By the way, did you know Geena Parcell is expecting again?"

Marcella gasped at the news of her friend. Geena had recently become a great friend, but between work and her relationship with Denver, she hadn't taken the time these past few weeks to contact her. "Geena is pregnant? Little George is only about two-and-a-half months old! Where did you hear this?"

"Annie told me yesterday. She said Geena just found out about it a few days ago. She says Vince is over the moon."

He would be, Marcella thought. Vince was crazy in love with Geena and she with him. They'd had their troubles in the past, but thankfully they were a beautiful married couple now.

"This is incredible," Marcella murmured thoughtfully. "Back when her first baby, Emma Rose, was born, I would hold her and think I'd never have another baby of my own. Now the two of us are going to have babies together!" She looked questioningly at her mother. "Does Geena know about me being pregnant?"

"Not that I'm aware of. Annie couldn't have told her because I haven't mentioned it to her or anyone."

Annie was a mutual friend whose house was situated between Marcella's and her mother's. The widow had been a longtime friend, along with being Emma Rose and George's babysitter.

"Thanks, Mother. I'm taking time off tomorrow to see my ob-gyn. I'll try to stop by Geena's when I'm finished."

"Good. It will lift your spirits to see her." She rose from the chair and walked across to where a plate of iced sugar cookies sat on the cabinet counter. "You stay right there. I'm bringing you some cookies and milk and you're going to down all of it without argument."

Marcella was about to tell her mother how she never quit being a waitress, when several loud thumps sounded from another part of the house. By the time she jumped to her feet, she could hear the boys shouting at each other.

Rushing through the house, she jerked open the bedroom door to see Harry and Peter rolling wildly on the floor, fists flying as they tried to pummel each other. The sight of the two boys locked in an angry wrestling match was shocking. They often teased and argued, but they'd never come to physical blows before now.

"Stop this! Stop it right now!" Marcella stopped herself just short of shouting the command.

Moving past her, Saundra picked up both boys by the collars of their pajamas and planted herself between them.

"What is going on with you two?" the older woman demanded.

Instead of answering their grandmother's question, the two boys glared resentfully at each other.

Feeling sick inside, Marcella stepped forward to see a long red mark above Peter's eye and a trickle of blood from one of Harry's nostrils. "Okay, guys, answer your grandmother's question. Right now!"

Peter was the first to capitulate, and when his lip began to tremble uncontrollably, Marcella had to resist the urge to gather him into her arms.

"Harry said Denver was a creep. That we'd never see

him again—that he was just like the daddies that didn't want us! That ain't true! Denver will see us again. I know he will," Peter cried defiantly. "'Cause he loves us."

"You're stupid, Peter!" Harry shouted at him. "Denver don't love us. He don't care if he ever sees us! We ain't nothing to him! Nothing!"

Tears streaming from his eyes, Peter attempted to throw another punch at his brother, but Marcella managed to grab his arm before it could do harm to anyone.

"That's enough, Peter! And, Harry, you should be ashamed for saying such things to your brother. You both should be ashamed for behaving like hooligans and hurting each other. Do you think Denver would be proud of your behavior?"

"Don't matter," Harry muttered in a surly voice. "He won't be around anyway."

Still defiant, Peter swiped at the tears on his cheeks. "He'd be proud of me 'cause I stuck up for him. I didn't call him no creep, either!"

Behind Marcella, her mother cleared her throat. "I'm going to let you handle this by yourself, daughter. I'll be in the kitchen if you need me."

Saundra left the room and quietly closed the door behind them. Marcella put a hand on each boy's shoulder and guided them over to a bed.

"Sit down here beside me," she instructed. "We're going to have a talk about Denver. And then I'm going to decide how to punish you both for fighting."

Twenty minutes later, Marcella walked into the living room, dabbing at her tears as she stood staring at the blue spruce sitting in one corner of the room. Over the years, she'd had Christmas trees look far worse than this one with its lopsided tinsel and drooping lights. The appearance of the tree was a perfect example of her life. She was still standing, but she didn't have much to feel proud about.

"So much for having a fun evening of tree trimming," she said glumly. "Instead, my boys end up in a boxing match."

From her seat on the couch, Saundra patted the cushion next to her. "Come here, honey."

Marcella crossed the room and gladly welcomed the comfort of her mother's arms. Even though Saundra was often too bossy and opinionated, she'd always been around to love and support Marcella through all the ups and downs.

Hugging Marcella tightly, she asked, "Are the boys calmed down now?"

Easing out of her mother's embrace, Marcella leaned back against the couch and let out a long sigh. "Yes. I cleaned up their faces and gave them a long talk. When I left their room, they were snuggled together in the same bed."

Her mother gave her a wan smile. "You and Spence used to do the same thing. One minute you'd be in a boxing match and the next you'd be hugging each other. It will all pass, honey."

Using her fingertips, Marcella massaged her furrowed brow. "I probably made a mistake, Mom. A few minutes ago I promised the boys I'd talk with Denver about spending some time with them. I honestly don't want to say a word to the man. But Peter and Harry need to understand this breakup is not their fault. Both of them have always believed their fathers deserted them because they weren't good enough or worthy of a father's love. Harry and Peter were just beginning to believe that Denver felt differently about them. And then…"

"Now Harry is hiding behind a tough-guy face and Peter is lashing out with his fists," Saundra finished ruefully, then turned a thoughtful glance on Marcella. "Did you tell them about the baby?"

"No. They have enough on their little minds without adding to it."

Saundra frowned. "But, honey, learning they're going to soon get a brother or sister might lift their spirits. And you're going to have to tell them before too long."

Before they start asking why their mom is growing a belly, Marcella thought helplessly. "I'm planning on telling them at Christmas. I keep thinking that maybe—"

When she broke off with an anguished sigh, her mother reached over and clasped her hand. "That maybe the cowboy will have a change of heart?"

Marcella's response was something between a sob and a groan. "Stupid of me, isn't it? I told him I never wanted to see him again. But my heart is still aching for him. After Gordon turned out to be a loser, I never thought I'd find myself feeling this way about any man."

"So you've forgiven Denver? You're going to forget he accused you of being deceitful and manipulative?" she asked.

The sarcasm in her mother's voice couldn't be missed. Marcella had to admit the sound mirrored the bitter feelings she'd been struggling to put behind her. "I have to forgive him, Mother. For the sake of my unborn child and my boys. And for my own sake."

Saundra shook her head. "You have far more mercy in you than I could ever have. So in other words, you're telling me you'd take him back?"

Marcella's short laugh was full of pain. "Don't worry, Mom. I don't see any chance of the two of us getting back together. When I first met Denver, he made it clear he

didn't want a wife or a child. I made the mistake of believing I was the woman he might change for—that he'd
feel different with me."

The next day saw clear blue skies and bright sun shin-
ing down on the ranch. That afternoon, when Denver
and Rafe rode their horses away from the ranch yard
and headed west, only patches of snow remained on the
ground. The wind had settled to a pleasant breeze and,
to be only a few days before Christmas, it was beautiful weather.

"I've made Griff and Ronnie mad at me," Rafe said as
the horses walked briskly abreast of each other. "They
wanted to do this chore themselves. You know Griff, if
he thinks there's going to be a little excitement, he wants
to be in on it."

Denver glanced to a rough ridge of hills to the far
southwest, where the two men expected to find a sick bull.
Their plan was to rope and secure him, then give him an
injection of long-lasting antibiotic. But the motley-colored
bull with crooked horns had a wild streak. Several times
Orin had threatened to sell the animal that the ranch hands
had dubbed Crowbait. But Rafe had become attached to
the ornery critter and, oddly enough, so had Denver. So
whenever Crowbait needed attention, Denver and Rafe
took on the dangerous responsibility of caring for him.

"I don't think we'll have much trouble with the ole
boy today." Denver tugged the brim of his black hat a
bit lower on his forehead. "Especially if he isn't feeling
his best."

"Hmmp. He just has a few sniffles, and that might
make him meaner. We'll see." Rafe glanced his way. "I
got busy yesterday and forgot to thank you for coming
to Dad's little get-together."

Denver shrugged. "I'm glad I did. It's good to see Orin so happy. Noreen has turned him into a different man."

Rafe nodded. "Damned right she has. You remember how Dad was after Mom died. He turned himself into a recluse and was behaving like an old man. Who would have thought he'd look sideways at a woman twenty years his junior? Just goes to show you how life can take unexpected turns."

Denver was well experienced with unexpected turns. He'd had plenty of them during his young life and now he was facing more. These past days since Marcella had told him about the baby, his whole world felt as if it was turning out of control. He wanted to stop the chaos in his head and the torment in his heart. But he didn't know how to start. Or even if he had the courage to try.

Rafe's chuckle interrupted Denver's dismal thoughts.

"Females are so hard to figure. For some unexplainable reason, little Colleen thinks you're Prince Charming. I've tried to tell her you ride a horse and get cow manure on your hands just like her daddy does. But that doesn't seem to dim her attraction for you. If this next baby is a girl, I'm not going to let you near her until she's a grown woman and old enough to see you're nothing but a grizzled cowboy," he joked.

This next baby. Rafe's words snagged Denver's attention and he looked over at his friend while wondering if he'd misunderstood.

"Uh—Rafe, you said next baby. Are you and Lilly planning on having another child?"

Grinning broadly, Rafe shook his head. "We're not thinking about it, Denver. We've already got the ball rolling. Lilly just made a trip to the doctor. She's about six weeks pregnant. I shouldn't be telling you—we haven't yet spread the news to the family. But what the heck, you're my best bud in the world. And I wanted you to know."

If circumstances had been different, Denver would've probably burst out laughing. He and his best friend having babies at the same time was too far-fetched to ever dream possible. Especially when Denver had never planned to have a child of his own. Period. And suddenly it all became too much for him to hold inside.

"Congratulations, Rafe. I'm happy for you. Really happy. And I—"

As he broke off, searching for the right words, Rafe drew his horse to a halt, forcing Denver to do the same.

"What's wrong?" Rafe asked. "You look half-sick or something. Look, man, Lilly is the one with the nausea. The word *pregnant* shouldn't put a green look on your face."

"Let's dismount," Denver said. "I need to talk to you."

Sensing the seriousness in Denver's voice, Rafe nodded and the two men climbed from their saddles.

Rafe pointed to an outcropping of rocks shaded by a large Joshua tree. "Let's go sit on those boulders over there."

With both horses trained to stay ground-tied, the two men simply let the reins down and left the animals where they stood.

At the boulders, Rafe brushed off a bit of snow, then sat on the cold rock. A short space over, Denver did the same.

"Okay," Rafe said, leveling a look on him. "Fire away. Are you trying to ask for a raise? If you are, you don't need to be so worried about it. I'm sure Dad will come through for you."

In spite of the misery inside him, Denver grunted a short laugh. "Oh Lord, Rafe, are you crazy? The salary

the Silver Horn pays me is so much it's practically in-
decent. Besides, don't you remember? Last year on my
birthday Orin gave me that share in one of his copper
mines. The dividends on that is paying me more money
than I know what to do with. No. Money is not the issue.
It's Marcella."

"Oh. So you're still thinking about her."

"Thinking about her!" Denver threw up his gloved
hands. "Rafe, you have no idea!"

"And I won't have an idea until you tell me," Rafe impatiently prodded.

Denver took a deep breath and expelled it. "Marcella
is pregnant with my baby."

For several long seconds a stunned expression was
frozen on Rafe's face, and then he let out a loud yelp of
joy. "You and Marcella. Me and Lilly. Having babies at
the same time? This is great! Really great!"

"For you, maybe. Things are a lot different for me."

"How do you mean?"

Denver sputtered. "Do I need to draw a picture? Lilly
is your wife. You already have two children."

Rafe shot him an impatient look. "That's supposed
to explain things? Marcella could be your wife. If you
wanted her to be. Then you'd have a wife and two kids,
too."

Snorting, Denver said in a tight voice, "Marcella isn't
speaking to me. She never wants to see me again. She
hardly wants to become my wife."

Rafe's eyes narrowed with speculation. "Do you want
her to be your wife?"

Swallowing at the hard lump in his throat, Denver
looked across the valley floor to the distant mountains.
"All these years since Christa died I never wanted to be
married again."

"You've said that much to me before," Rafe said. "And for a long time I thought it was because you were still grieving over the woman you lost. Though these past few years I'm not so sure. Dad thought Mom was the only woman on this earth, but even he's managed to move on. You haven't."

Denver had to choke out his next words, and he hated showing this vulnerable side of himself to Rafe. But he was tired of always being the strong, sturdy one. Tired of hiding the pain he'd carried with him for so long. "It's not just getting over losing a wife, Rafe. I…I lost a baby, too."

Rafe studied him for long moments and Denver expected him to come out with the standard *I'm sorry*, or *how terrible*. Instead, he surprised him by saying, "I wish you had told me this years ago."

"Why?" Denver asked dourly. "What good would that have done?"

"Sharing your burdens makes the load a lot lighter to bear, Denver."

"It's something that hurts to talk about—to even think about," Denver tried to reason. "You see, Christa wasn't supposed to get pregnant. Her condition made it far too risky. But she went behind my back and quit taking her birth control pills. She died carrying my baby."

"Did you tell Marcella about this?" Rafe asked.

Denver nodded. "She assured me that nothing would happen to her. That she wouldn't get pregnant. But she did. And I—well, when she told me she was carrying our child, I couldn't handle it. I ended up saying some awful things to her."

Rafe's jaw dropped as he stared at Denver in disbelief. "Awful things? Are you crazy, Denver? Marcella is one of the sweetest, most gentle souls on this earth. You should have been smothering her with kisses. Down on your knees thanking her for giving you a child. What were you thinking?"

Heaving out a long breath, Denver stood and jammed his gloved hands in his coat pockets. "I wasn't. I couldn't think, Rafe! Suddenly I was seeing Christa in the hospital hooked up to all sorts of tubes and machines as the doctors tried to save her and the baby. I was remembering how she cheated us out of the chance to have a life together."

Rafe remained quiet for so long that Denver decided his friend had nothing else to say. But finally he rose to his feet and walked over to stand in front of Denver. The expression on his friend's face was nothing close to empathetic; it was downright angry.

"You can't forgive your late wife for deceiving you and even dying on you, so you take all that bitterness out on Marcella." He snorted with disgust. "I don't blame Marcella for never wanting to see you again. You don't deserve her or her sons."

"All right! Beat me up! You think that will make me feel any worse than I already do?" Denver practically shouted at him. "When Marcella told me she was pregnant, I went into a cold shock. I couldn't even remember driving back to the ranch. And then when I finally got part of my senses back, I realized I was scared to death. I'm still scared to death!"

He grabbed the front of Rafe's coat and gently shook him for answers. "What if something happens to Marcella? To the baby? I couldn't stand it again, Rafe."

Rafe clamped a hand on Denver's shoulder and said in a steadying voice, "Anything can happen. At any time. That's life, Denver. I lost my sister Darci when she was only two. I was five at the time and I considered her my little buddy. After she died, I clung to my mother for a long, long time. I was afraid to let her out of my sight. Afraid Mom would leave me, too. Eventually, she also died, and that was tragic. But I, and the rest of my family, had to move on. A person can't live their whole life in fear. That's not really living. Just ask Dad."

Denver dropped his head and stared at the cold ground. In a few months the patches of snow would be gone. Grass would sprout and sage would bloom. The arrival of his child would be growing nearer, and Denver wanted to be there to welcome it into the world and his arms. He wanted to be with Marcella. Not just as a man who'd fathered her baby, but as a husband who loved her deeply.

He lifted his head. "I've been wrong, Rafe. No— change that to guilty. I shouldn't have relied on Christa to be solely responsible for birth control. I should've used my own to make certain she wouldn't get pregnant. As for Marcella, God help me, but I think deep down I ignored the responsibility because I...wanted a baby with her. But then when her pregnancy became an actuality, I panicked."

Rafe nodded soberly. "I can understand that. It's a jolt for a man to hear he's going to be a father. Even when the event is planned. It's a big responsibility to be given a tiny human being that can't talk or walk and you have to help it grow into a man or a woman. I get it, Denver. In your case, I really do understand your fears."

Denver shook his head. "I'm not a coward, Rafe. I've got to make this right with Marcella. I love her."

Rafe's faint smile was all-knowing. "You didn't have to tell me that. I can see it all over your face." He gave Denver's shoulder an encouraging slap. "Come on, let's mount up. We still have Crowbait to deal with. And when we get back to the ranch, I want you to hightail it to town and find Marcella. Even if you have to go to the ER to do it."

Less than a half hour later, they found the motley bull in a muddy ravine barely wide enough to ride the horses through. As soon as the ornery animal spotted them, he took off at a defiant trot.

Eventually, Crowbait decided the ravine wasn't a place he wanted to be with two horses on his tail. When he climbed onto open land, Denver quickly maneuvered his horse close enough to rope the bull's horns. Rafe followed and snagged a loop around the animal's heels. Once they had the bull safely secured on the ground, Denver retrieved medication from a satchel tied to the back of his saddle.

After he injected the antibiotic under the bull's tough skin, he patted his neck. "There, ole boy. By this time tomorrow your sniffles will just about be gone."

"Yeah, maybe he'll send us a thank-you card," Rafe joked. "Right now, he's pretty damned angry. Once we take these lariats off him, we're going to have to run like hell."

"I'm ready if you are," Denver told him. "Let's do it!"

Rafe uncoiled the rope from the bull's heels while Denver gingerly eased the loop off the wide set of horns.

Freed from the confines, the bull jumped to his feet. While he shook the mud from his hide, Denver and Rafe raced toward the horses.

Behind them the bull began to bellow loudly, and both men glanced anxiously over their shoulders to see the bull pawing the ground, sending mud and snow flying in the air.

"He's going to charge, Denver!" Rafe shouted. "We can't make it to the horses! Run for those rocks over there!"

Struggling against the bulky weight of their chaps and boots, the two men raced toward a pile of large boulders, but they weren't fast enough. Before they could reach safety, Crowbait took aim and rammed Denver square in the back. The impact tossed him several feet in the air, before he landed like a rag doll near a bed of prickly pear.

The next thing Denver knew, his face was pressed into the dirt and a hot, piercing pain was spreading up and down his side. Half-conscious, he could hear Rafe behind him, yelling at the bull, then a set of hoofbeats striking the ground. If the bull charged the horses, they would definitely run and leave him and Rafe afoot. The frantic thought rushed through his dazed mind and he tried to lift himself up to look, but the pain in his side wouldn't allow him to move.

Suddenly Rafe was lifting his head off the ground and propping it on his thigh. "Denver! Can you hear me?"

Denver opened his eyes and tried to draw in a breath, but very little air seemed to fill his lungs.

"Rafe," he said in a wheezy voice. "Is the bull gone?"

"Yes, he's run off. Afraid I'd shoot him, no doubt. He'd better be damned glad I didn't have my rifle with me!"

"No! Leave him...alone," Denver said between gasps for breaths. "He was only trying to...protect himself."

Jerking a bandanna from the back pocket of his jeans, Rafe started wiping dirt and bits of vegetation from Denver's face. "Oh God, are you hurt badly?"

"I don't know. I can hardly breathe. I think I've broken a rib or something. Are the horses still here?"

"Yeah. They're the best two buddies we ever had. Most horses would've headed for the heels when Crowbait went crazy." Satisfied he'd gotten most of the dirt off Denver's face, he quickly unbuttoned his coat. "Let me take a look. We need to know if you're bleeding."

After locating his hat, Rafe stuffed it beneath Denver's head for a pillow, then turned his attention to the wound in his side. Even the movement of easing back the shirt fabric sent shards of pain up and down Denver's rib cage.

"The flesh hasn't been broken," he reported. "I guess the padding of your coat prevented that from happening. But there's a huge blue lump starting to form. We've got to get you back to the ranch and to the doctor as soon as possible. If your rib has punctured a lung, that could be mighty serious."

"Just get me to my horse," Denver told him. "I can make it."

"Hell no! I'm going to ride back for help."

Denver muttered a curse. "What kind of help? No vehicle can get back here."

"A four-wheeler can make it."

"Skipper can give me a far smoother ride than a damned four-wheeler. Now quit arguing and help me up."

Rafe helped him to a sitting position, then went after the horses. Once Skipper was standing directly next to Denver, Rafe helped him to his feet. By the time he climbed into the saddle, he was very close to passing out from the pain.

"Damn it, this is crazy!" Rafe protested. "You can't make it all the way back to the ranch! We're several miles out! You might be bleeding inside."

"Give me the reins," Denver ordered through clenched teeth. "Let's get out of here. I've got to get to town—to see Marcella."

"Let's just both pray you make it back to the Silver Horn," Rafe said worriedly. "Seeing Marcella will have to come later."

Chapter Thirteen

Marcella was standing at the main desk in the ER, chatting with Helen and a few other nurses, when she noticed Dr. Whitehorse stepping off a nearby elevator. Since he rarely appeared in this portion of the hospital, she hoped his business downstairs was professional and not an attempt to see her. Several times this past week their paths had crossed in unexpected places around the hospital, making her wonder whether the incidents had been coincidental or planned.

Tall, dark and solidly built, the physician was definitely handsome. He also possessed a kind, gentle manner that instantly put a person at ease. But as much as Marcella had always liked the man, he didn't make her heart go zing or bells ring in her head. Only Denver had that unexplainable effect on her.

Denver. Dear Lord, what was she going to do about him? The past few days had dimmed her anger. Now tears remained a constant threat at the backs of her eyes, while a hollow ache of longing weighed heavy in her chest. Tonight after work, she had to pick up her phone and call him. He might not want to see her again, but she had to somehow convince him that the boys needed him.

She needed him. Their life together shouldn't be over. It should just be beginning.

The nudge of an elbow in her ribs interrupted Marcella's whirling thoughts and she looked over to see Paige grinning cleverly at her.

"Uh—I think Dr. Hunky is heading this way and he has his eyes set on you. Why don't you go say hello and put him out of his misery?"

From the corner of her eye, Marcella could see the doctor fast approaching.

"Why don't *you* go say hello to him?" Marcella suggested.

Paige chuckled. "Because he doesn't like coarse country girls like me."

Biting back an impatient sigh, Marcella stepped away from the group to intercept the good doctor before he reached the nurses' desk. If he wanted to speak with her, at least she could prevent the conversation from reaching a bunch of attentive ears.

"Hello, Dr. Whitehorse."

He smiled warmly, and Marcella thought back to the last time she'd seen that sort of smile on Denver's face. It had happened only moments before she'd told him about the baby. And she very much doubted he'd smiled since.

"Hello, Marcella. How are you?"

"I'm fine. Thank you for asking. If you're here in the ER to check on a patient, we just sent the last one to X-ray. We're actually getting a little breather this afternoon. I hope you don't think we nurses stand around talking most of the day."

His smile deepened. "I've seen the ER in action. You deserve every breather you can get." He glanced over her shoulder at the other nurses, then refocused his attention on her face. "Actually, I came down here to the ER hoping I could have a moment or two with you."

Even though Paige and a few other nurses had teased her about Dr. Whitehorse wanting to date her, she'd never put much stock in the talk. Until now.

"Oh. Is there something I can help you with?"

A shy smile crossed the doctor's face. "I'm hoping you can. The Fallon Reservation will be having special Christmas festivities this coming weekend. If all goes well with my schedule, I plan to attend Saturday. It would be a lot merrier for me if you'd accompany me for the day."

Even though she should've been expecting it, his invitation caught her completely off guard. At the most, she was thinking he wanted her to join him for a cup of coffee in the cafeteria lounge. Not a day of celebration with his Native family.

Her mind was whirling, searching for the best way to handle the situation, when a hopeful grin crossed his face.

"It's the holiday season. Time to have a little fun. And I like you, Marcella. I'm pretty sure you've figured that out by now."

She could feel her face turning warm with embarrassment. "I like you, too, Dr. Whitehorse. But I—well, right now I'm—"

When she broke off awkwardly, the doctor surprised her by taking her by the arm and leading her to a spot across the room.

"First of all, my name is James. Jay to my friends. And you don't have to give me any explanations. I've heard about the baby. And that things haven't exactly worked out with the father."

Marcella's mouth fell open. By now, most of the nurses she worked with in the ER had heard about her condition and her breakup with Denver. But she hadn't expected any of them to start blabbing the news.

"Who told you that?"

He shook his head. "Not Paige, if that's what you're thinking. It doesn't matter who. Hospital gossip spreads faster than the flu virus."

The doctor was right. Nothing personal stayed that way for long around here. She shouldn't let the chatter bother her. In a couple more months her condition would begin to show to anyone who bothered to look at her. Besides, she was proud of her coming baby. It was a special part of her and Denver, and she would always be grateful that something wonderful came out of their union.

Lifting her chin, she said, "Then you'll probably understand I'm not exactly in the holiday spirit. You should ask someone who would be a fun date for you. Not me."

He took her hand and squeezed it, and Marcella wished she could have felt something more than the simple touch from a friend.

James Whitehorse gave her an understanding smile. "I don't expect you to laugh or dance or tell jokes all day long. There'll be all sorts of good things to eat and you can see some of the culture of the Paiute and Shoshone tribes."

This coming weekend was the annual Christmas barn party on the Silver Horn Ranch. It was always a huge celebration with a live band, lots of dancing, mounds of rich food and presents for everyone. Normally, Marcella would be attending, but this year she was staying away from the ranch. Seeing Denver among the partygoers would simply be too painful.

"I'll think about it, Jay," she told him. "And let you know by tomorrow morning."

"Great! I—"

The doctor paused as Paige suddenly called to her from the corridor leading into the treatment area.

"Marcella! Over here, hurry! It's Denver!"

Denver? Icy fear shot through her, and not bothering to excuse herself to the doctor, she took off in a run toward the nurses' desk.

Meeting her halfway, Paige latched a hand onto Marcella's shoulder and guided her toward the treatment area.

Her heart frantically racing, Marcella asked, "What's happened?"

"Don't panic," Paige swiftly ordered. "He's not critical. At least, he doesn't appear to be. One of the Calhouns brought him in. Rafe, I believe—he's in the waiting area."

"Where is Denver?"

By now they'd reached the main room of the ER, and Paige pointed to a compartment shielded by heavy white curtains.

"Dr. Sherman is with him now," she told her while keeping her hand firmly planted on Marcella's arm. "I'm not sure you should go in there. Let me handle it."

"Not on your life!" Marcella exclaimed, then hurried into the compartment.

"It's about time someone showed up!" the doctor practically shouted as he attempted to push Denver's shirt away from his chest. "Where is Nurse Winters?"

"Outside—"

"Tell her to get herself in here!"

Marcella didn't have to bother going after Paige; the nurse appeared instantly and the two of them jumped into action removing Denver's shirt and acquiring his vitals. As they moved his upper body one way and then another, his eyes were squeezed tightly shut, his teeth clenched with pain.

After a quick scan of Denver's vitals, the doctor began to examine the large contusion on Denver's lower rib cage. "He needs oxygen and IV," he ordered, quickly adding the specifics of each. "That means now! Not tomorrow!"

Her hands shaking, Marcella pulled the necessary items for the IV from a nearby cabinet and returned to the bedside. Up until now Denver's eyes had been closed, but the moment she touched his arm, his lids flew open and a pair of brown orbs looked straight at her.

"Marcella!"

Even though her name came out as a raspy whisper, there was a tender plea in it that very nearly had Marcella bursting into tears.

"Do you know this man?"

Paige answered Dr. Sherman's question before Marcella had the chance.

"He's the father of her baby."

There was a momentary pause, but Marcella didn't bother glancing over to see whether the ER physician was about to order her out of the treatment area. She continued on with her job of finding a suitable vein for the IV.

Finally, Dr. Sherman replied, "Then we'd better take extra good care of him."

The unexpected show of kindness from the testy physician had Paige slicing her a look of disbelief. Meanwhile, Marcella warned Denver, "Sorry. You're going to feel a stick."

Denver tried to grunt out a laugh, but the pain in his side stopped him short. "My leg," he said. "It's full of prickly pear spines. Another stick isn't going to hurt."

"Nurse Winters, cut his jeans open and we'll see about the spines." He asked Denver, "How did this happen? What hit you? Or you hit what?"

"A mean bull with long horns. We were doctoring him

and he charged," Denver explained gruffly. "He knocked me off my feet. My partner said I flew through the air. I don't know. The next thing I knew I was on the ground and could hardly breathe."

A cold shiver ran down Marcella's spine. He could've been killed, paralyzed or, at the least, disabled for months. The reality jolted her. If she hadn't realized just how important this man was to her life before, she certainly knew it now.

"Hmm. That explains things." Dr. Sherman placed the disc of the stethoscope against Denver's chest and listened intently at several different spots. Eventually, he stated, "You must be a lucky guy. Your lung doesn't seem to be punctured. And from this initial assessment, you don't appear to have any internal bleeding, but you definitely have some broken ribs. I'm sending you to the lab for an X-ray and an MRI to see exactly what sort of damage is involved. Once I look at the pictures, I'll determine whether you'll need more hospital care or if I can tape you and send you home."

By now Marcella had the IV ready and Paige had a tube of oxygen flowing into Denver's nose. The doctor rattled off several drugs to be administered, then scribbled orders on a clipboard before motioning to Paige.

"Nurse Winters, quit dallying around and come with me."

He started out of the curtained cubicle and Paige called out to him, "But, Doctor, the spines in his legs!"

He shot her a tired look. "Marcella is perfectly capable of dealing with the patient's leg. Now get out of there! I need your help elsewhere."

As soon as the doctor and nurse disappeared from the small treatment area, Denver said, "He calls you

Marcella and her Nurse Winters. Does he always talk to her like that?"

Marcella nodded while her heart squeezed with pain. He looked so bruised and beaten, yet so very, very dear. It didn't matter what he'd said to her in the past or how he'd said it. All she wanted was to take away his pain, to tell him how much she wanted them to be together. But would he ever feel the same way?

Clearing her throat, she said, "Dr. Sherman goes out of his way to hide his real feelings from Paige."

"Like someone else I know," he murmured soberly.

Marcella moved to the head of the bed, and he wrapped a hand around her forearm. Her eyes full of moisture, she leaned her head down to his.

"Are you trying to make a point?" she asked, not allowing herself to think past the moment, or to hope there might be a chance for them.

"It means all those awful things I said to you about the pregnancy—I was trying to hide my real feelings, too."

As his words slowly sank in, her head swung back and forth in disbelief. "You had to be gored by a bull to tell me this?"

He grimaced. "I wasn't gored. The horn didn't rip into me!"

The fear that had poured through her when she'd first seen him on the gurney had left her shaken to the core. To hear him make light of the accident angered her.

She pointed to the large blue contusion rising up on his rib cage. "Look at this! That's close to being gored. You could've been killed!"

"Would you have cared?" he asked softly.

The moisture in her eyes spilled onto her cheeks and she quickly dashed it away and sniffed. "A nurse isn't supposed to show her emotions in front of a patient, but I happen to…love this patient."

Amazement joined the pain on his face. "Marcella! Do you really mean what you just said?"

She gazed into his brown eyes and the protective shell around her heart fell away, leaving her raw emotions exposed and throbbing like an open wound. "I mean it. Although I'm not sure why."

He started to push his upper body off the gurney, but Marcella grabbed his shoulders and gently lowered him back to the narrow bed.

"Don't try," she ordered softly.

"But there are things I need to say—"

Her throat tight, she shook her head. "Right now I have to get your meds going. Then we'll talk."

Marcella hurried away to the drug dispensary. When she returned, she was relieved to see that a bit of color had returned to Denver's face, telling her the oxygen was doing its job.

As she hung the IV bag and connected the line to the port in his arm, he asked, "Can you tell me what's in that bag? A bunch of truth serum?"

Ignoring his attempt at a joke, Marcella concentrated on adjusting the drip. "Everything you need to get well is in this solution," she answered sagely.

"That's not true. Everything I need is standing right here beside me."

Afraid to give in to the rays of hope bursting inside her, she turned to him. "Have you forgotten I'm pregnant with your baby? A baby you don't want."

Once again he attempted to rise up, but his shoulders managed to lift only a few inches before he let out a defeated groan and fell back to the mattress. "Don't say that, Marcella. Don't ever think it or say it! I want our baby and you! More than anything."

"So when did you come to this conclusion?" she asked, the misery of the past several days edging her voice with sarcasm. "When you thought you might die from your injury?"

He mouthed several curse words while snatching a hold on her hand. "I never thought I was going to die! You're probably not going to believe this. But before the incident with the bull, I had decided to drive into town today to see you—to beg you to forgive me. I'd already told Rafe. I hardly planned for Crowbait to run me down or knew that I would end up meeting you like this in the ER."

She leaped on one important word. "Did I hear you right? Did you say *forgive* you?"

A sheepish look swept over his features. "You heard me. I'm asking you to forgive me. For acting like a jackass of the worst kind. I didn't want to hurt you."

"But you did. You hurt me terribly." She swallowed at the ache in her throat. "Look, Denver, I can accept the fact that you don't love me. I can even understand your reluctance to enter into another marriage. But to deliberately accuse me of getting pregnant like your first wife... that was—is—too much!"

His expression rueful, he shook his head. "You're wrong, my darling! So wrong. I do love you. More than anything. I do want to be your husband. I think I've wanted that from the very start. But from the moment we began growing close, I turned into a coward. The more I loved you, the more frightened I got. That morning when you told me about the baby, I was suddenly terrified. All I could think about was you dying—the baby dying. I wanted to tear into you for risking everything precious we had together. I reacted like an idiot. But to be honest, I didn't know half of what I was doing or saying."

Suddenly none of it mattered anymore. Denver loved her. And she loved him. There would be bright, beautiful days ahead for them.

Tears streaming down her face, she leaned over and gently smoothed the dark tousled hair off his brow. "I've hardly behaved in the best of ways, either, Denver. And you might not believe it, but I had decided to call you as soon as my shift ended. I was going to plead my case for us to be together—whether you wanted to hear it or not. The last thing I expected was to see you lying here in the ER with broken ribs!"

A weary smile tilted the corners of his lips. "I've missed you so much. You and the boys."

She sighed as joy began to flood through her, washing away all the doubts and sadness she'd carried with her since she'd ordered him out of her life. "We've missed you, too. Very much."

His gaze flickered up to hers. "Have you told them about the baby yet?"

Shaking her head, she said, "I was planning to tell them at Christmas. After all, the baby is a gift. Against giant odds, he was miraculously conceived. He'll be born healthy and handsome. You have to keep that faith and hold it in your heart. And then you won't be frightened anymore. I won't let you be."

A sly smile lit his brown eyes. "He? Maybe it's a she with bright red hair and a fiery temperament. Did that idea ever cross your mind?"

"I'm thinking it might be another son with dark hair and warm brown eyes. Would you like to have a daughter?" she asked softly.

"Daughter. Son. Either way, I'll love it with all my heart. I want us to have babies, Marcella. As many as you want. That's what I'd like."

Bending, she placed a tender kiss on his lips. Once she raised her head, she was touched by the sheen of moisture glazing his eyes.

He said, "When the nurse first wheeled me back here, I saw you talking with a good-looking guy. The way he was touching your arm—he was acting like the two of you were mighty familiar."

Her brows lifted coyly. "That was Dr. Whitehorse. He just happened to be asking me for a date—to a Christmas celebration."

His expression turned suspicious, which only made Marcella give him a taunting grin.

"A date?" he asked cautiously. "Does he know you're pregnant?"

Marcella chuckled softly. "Yes. But he's a very good man. He'd never hold that against a woman."

Frowning now, Denver grunted. "What did you tell him?"

"I told him I'd call him in the morning and give him my answer."

He squeezed her hand. "And what's your answer going to be?"

She brought her lips against his and whispered, "That I already have a date with another man. A date for the rest of my life."

His hand cupped the back of her neck; he brought her mouth fully down on his and was still kissing her when a voice sounded behind them.

"Uh—sorry. Is this the patient that's headed to X-ray?"

Marcella stepped back from the gurney to see two male orderlies waiting to wheel Denver back to Radiology.

"He's all yours," she said happily. "Just make sure you bring him right back here to me."

Epilogue

Marcella awoke on Christmas morning snuggled next to her husband's warm body. Beyond the bed, through the partially opened curtains, she could see that a dusting of snow had fallen the night before, decorating the backyard and steep hill beyond with white tinsel.

With a sigh of contentment, she climbed from the bed and pulled on a deep green robe she'd purchased especially for this day. She was tying the silky sash at her waist when the sparkle of the large diamond on her finger caught her eye, and for a brief moment she stared in wonder at the ring and all that it symbolized.

To everyone's relief, Denver's injury from the bull had turned out to be nothing more than bruised and broken ribs. He was still dealing with a major amount of pain and would do so for several more weeks until they healed, but he hadn't let that deter their plans to be married before Christmas.

Two days ago, they'd exchanged vows in a hastily thrown together ceremony in the same Carson City church she'd attended since she was a small child. Lilly, Ava and Paige had decorated the sanctuary with pink, red and white poinsettias against branches of evergreen.

Marcella had worn a lacy dress of pale pink with a knee-length hem. A short veil attached to a band of pearls had adorned her red hair.

Her mother, who'd been surprisingly happy about her daughter's marriage, had told her she'd never looked more radiant. As far as Marcella was concerned, her appearance had nothing to do with her dress or upswept hair, or even the string of pearls Lilly had lent her to wear. No, Marcella knew it was the sheer happiness of marrying the father of her coming child that had put an iridescent glow on her face.

Since the wedding, the days had passed in a happy but hectic whirl. With Denver's injury preventing him from doing anything but limited activity, a few of the ranch hands had volunteered to move everything from Marcella's house in town to Denver's home on the ranch. Her mother and Paige had helped her unpack most of the boxes and organize the rooms to accommodate her and the boys' belongings. But with such little time to prepare for Christmas, she'd had to leave some things still unpacked in order to finish her holiday shopping.

Somehow she'd gotten the gifts purchased and wrapped, but there was no tree to put them under. The pitiful little tree she and the boys had decorated in town couldn't have survived the thirty-plus-mile trip to the ranch, so she'd donated it to a downtown charity. And with Denver injured, he couldn't go out and cut one.

Last evening they were debating whether to drive into town to purchase another tree when Rafe and Lilly unexpectedly arrived with a beautiful Douglas fir and more than enough decorations to make it a real Christmas tree. Marcella had been overwhelmed with their thoughtfulness. But Rafe had insisted it was the least he could do to make up for the damage Crowbait had inflicted on his partner.

"What are you doing up?" Denver asked groggily. "Come back to bed and keep me warm."

Laughing, she tugged the cover off him. "It's Christmas, sleepyhead! Wake up! You have two sons who are probably already up and champing at the bit to open their gifts!"

His eyes flew wide-open. "The boys! Christmas!"

Before Marcella could remind him to remember his ribs, he started to roll out of bed.

Grabbing his side, he doubled over in pain. "Oh! Why do I forget about these damned ribs?"

"You're not used to being injured." She threw an arm across the back of his shoulders. "Let me help you off the bed."

The pain receded enough for him to give her a feeble grin. "Yes, Nurse Beautiful. I'll gladly accept your assistance."

"Beautiful for sure," she protested. "A bare face and tangled hair. You're seeing what your wife really looks like now."

Once he was steady on his feet, he bent his head and kissed her. "I see I'm the luckiest man on earth. Merry Christmas, darling. Help me into my jeans and we'll go find our boys."

Expecting to find Harry and Peter in the living room, they were surprised to see it empty and all the gifts under the tree undisturbed.

"We had a late night with the tree trimming," Denver reasoned. "Maybe they're still asleep."

Marcella cocked her head toward a faint sound coming from the kitchen. "I hear them. They must be feeding the cats."

"On Christmas morning? With gifts waiting under the tree? I've got to see this!" Denver exclaimed.

When they reached the open doorway leading into the kitchen, they spotted Harry and Peter, still in their pajamas, hovering over a tray holding two coffee mugs.

"I think we should stir Mom's," Peter told his brother. "She always stirs it after she puts in the cream."

"We don't need to stir Denver's, though," Harry pointed out. "'Cause he don't put anything in his."

"How do you know?" Peter asked. "He might put sugar in it."

With the seriousness of a chemist fretting over a formula, Harry shook his head. "I watched last night. He drinks the yucky stuff without anything in it."

Peter appeared convinced. "Okay. We'll take it to 'em just like this."

Exchanging amused glances, Marcella and Denver stepped forward, both of them shouting Merry Christmas.

After their initial surprise, the two boys raced to their parents and hugged them tightly. If Denver felt any pain from the show of affection, he didn't reveal it. Instead, he scrubbed both of them on the head while giving Marcella a conspiring wink.

"We think it's time to open our gifts," he told them. "But that can't happen until the cats are fed."

"We've already done that!" Harry exclaimed.

"Yeah! See, they're still eating." Peter pointed to a far corner of the room where the four cats were lined up at their saucers. Miraculously the group of felines had integrated without too much hissing and clawing.

Harry went to the table and picked up the tray. "We've made you coffee, too."

"For a special Christmas treat," Peter added proudly.

Genuinely impressed, Marcella exclaimed, "Wow! I think our sons really deserve some gifts now, don't you, Denver?"

"I sure do," he agreed. "I'll carry the coffee. Everybody head to the tree!"

In the living room, Marcella and Denver sat snuggled together on the couch, sipping their coffee, while watching Peter and Harry rip into their gifts. Sports gear, electronic games, and boots and hats from their new dad were all declared awesome stuff by both boys. But when they continued to avoid the big box pushed slightly behind the tree, Denver finally had to ask, "Why aren't you guys opening the big gift? It's to both of you. Don't you want to see what it is?"

"We wanted to save it for last," Peter said.

"Yeah," Harry added. "We figured it must be something special."

Marcella latched onto Denver's hand. "It is something very special. So you guys tear into it!"

Once the pair had the wrapping paper and cardboard box piled to one side, both boys stood staring with confusion at the wooden cradle.

"Is this a bed or something?" Harry asked. "It rocks!"

Peter turned a confused look on his parents. "Is this for the cats to sleep in?"

Denver burst out laughing, while Marcella left the couch to pick up the unopened card the boys had discarded on the floor.

"Here," she said, thrusting the card at the pair. "You were supposed to open this and read it."

Harry quickly ripped into the envelope and read aloud, "'This cradle is for your new baby brother or sister when he or she gets here this summer.'"

Silence stretched as Peter stared in wonder at his mother, and Harry's mouth formed a huge O.

"A brother or sister!" Harry finally shouted. "That's awesome!"

Peter went to his mother and placed his hand on her arm. "Mom, are you gonna have a baby?"

"That's right," she said gently. "Aren't you glad, too?"

"Yeah! I've been wanting a brother or sister for a long time. But..." His words trailed away as his doubtful gaze landed on Denver.

Marcella noticed that Harry had also taken on a worried expression as he glanced toward Denver.

"What's wrong with you boys?" Marcella asked. "We thought you'd be thrilled."

By now Denver had managed to push himself off the couch and walk over to where the three of them were standing next to the baby cradle.

He said, "Listen, you two, if you're worried your mother and I are going to give all our attention to the new baby and none to you, that just isn't going to happen."

Stepping forward, Peter bent his head back and gazed up at Denver. "You might not want to be our dad then. You might just want to be a dad to the new baby."

Denver glanced at Marcella, then turned to the boys and held out his arms. "Come here, guys."

Once he had an arm curved around each boy's shoulders, he pulled them close to his side. "I want to make something very clear to you both right now. You two will always be my sons. From this day on, I'm not Denver anymore. I'm Dad. And I don't want either one of you to forget it. We're all going to be a family. Together—for always. Okay?"

Clearly relieved, both boys shouted in unison, "Yeah, Dad!"

Peter looked up at the father he'd desperately wanted and grinned. "Does this mean we can let the cats sleep in the cradle until the baby gets here?"

Marcella groaned loudly while she watched Denver try to hold back a smile.

"No! No cats in the cradle! Now, both of you hop to it and get all this mess cleaned up! We're going up to the big ranch house for Christmas dinner and we don't want to be late."

A few minutes later, after the boys had cleaned up the wrappings and sat in the middle of the living room floor examining all their gifts, Marcella went in search of Denver and found him standing in the middle of the spare bedroom.

As she walked closer, she could hear him singing something soft and lyrical under his breath. "Darling, what are you doing in here by yourself?" She looped her arm through his. "It sounded like you were singing something."

A wry grin touched his face. "That's an old cowboy lullaby my mother used to sing to me and my sister. I'm surprised I still remember the words."

"I'm happy that your parents and sister were excited about the news of our marriage and the baby. Hopefully we can visit them soon," she told him.

"Mom, Dad and my sister never pressed me about getting married again or having kids. But when I told them about you and the boys and the baby, I could tell it was something they'd all been wanting for me for a long time." He looked down at her, his brown eyes full of love. "Yes, we'll go see them soon. I think Harry and Peter would enjoy a trip to Wyoming to see the ranch where their father grew up."

Touched deeply by this tender side of him, she pressed her cheek against his arm and sighed. "This is going to make a lovely nursery."

"I was just looking, thinking about all the changes we're going to make. And the furnishings we're going to put in here. Besides the cradle," he added teasingly.

Since she married Denver, she'd learned, much to her surprise, that he was a fairly wealthy man. And though she would never take advantage of the fact, she didn't try to discourage him from spending money on her or the boys, or their coming baby. She realized it was important to him to give his family the things they needed. And it was important for her to graciously accept them.

"All I ask is that you put a wooden rocker right in front of the windows," she told him while pointing to the perfect spot. "That way I can look out at the mountains while I rock our baby."

He kissed the top of her head. "Hmm. You're an easy woman to please."

She looked up at him and smiled. "You know, we were so busy buying the boys' Christmas gifts we forgot to get each other something."

His brown eyes filled with love as his hand came to rest on her lower belly. "We've already given each other a very special gift. Don't you agree?"

"Very special indeed." Her eyes delved deeply into his. "You're not worried anymore, are you? About me and the baby?"

His hand gently cupped the side of her face. "No.

You've taught me that life is too precious to waste it worrying. From now on it's all about believing and loving."

Like the happy sound of sleigh bells ringing across a field of crusty snow, joy filled her heart with music. This Christmas her cowboy had found the courage to sing his coming baby a lullaby, and her prayers for a family had finally been answered.

* * * * *

*Want to see what happens when
Paige Winters and Dr. Sherman
finally let the sparks fly?*

The next book in the MEN OF THE WEST
*miniseries will be available in May 2017
from Harlequin Special Edition.*

And don't miss previous books in the miniseries:
HIS BADGE, HER BABY...THEIR FAMILY?
HER RUGGED RANCHER
CHRISTMAS ON THE SILVER HORN RANCH
DADDY WORE SPURS

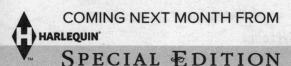

COMING NEXT MONTH FROM

HARLEQUIN®

SPECIAL EDITION

Available December 20, 2016

#2521 A FORTUNE IN WAITING
The Fortunes of Texas: The Secret Fortunes • by Michelle Major
Everyone in Austin is charmed by architect Keaton Fortune Whitfield, the sexy
new British Fortune in town—except Francesca Harriman, waitress at Lola May's
and the one woman he wants in his life! Can he win the heart of the beautiful
hometown girl?

#2522 TWICE A HERO, ALWAYS HER MAN
Matchmaking Mamas • by Marie Ferrarella
When popular news reporter Elliana King interviews Colin Benteen, a local police
detective, she had no idea this was the man who tried to save her late husband's
life—nor did she realize that he would capture her heart.

#2523 THE COWBOY'S RUNAWAY BRIDE
Celebration, TX • by Nancy Robards Thompson
Lady Chelsea Ashford Alden was forced to flee London after her fiancé
betrayed her, and now seeks refuge with her best friend in Celebration. When
Ethan Campbell catches her climbing in through a window, he doesn't realize the
only thing Chelsea will be stealing is his heart...

#2524 THE MAKEOVER PRESCRIPTION
Sugar Falls, Idaho • by Christy Jeffries
Baseball legend Kane Chatterson has tried hard to fly under the radar since
his epic scandal—until a beautiful society doctor named Julia Fitzgerald comes
along and throws him a curveball! She may be a genius, but men were never her
strong suit. Who better than the former MVP of the dating scene to help her out?

#2525 WINNING THE NANNY'S HEART
The Barlow Brothers • by Shirley Jump
When desperate widower Sam Millwright hires Katie Williams to be his nanny, he
finds a way back to his kids—and a second chance at love.

#2526 HIS BALLERINA BRIDE
Drake Diamonds • by Teri Wilson
Former ballerina and current jewelry designer Ophelia Rose has caught the eye
of the new CEO of Drake Diamonds, Artem Drake, but she has more secrets than
the average woman. A kitten, the ballet and *lots* of diamonds might just help
these two lonely souls come together in glitzy, snowy New York City.

**YOU CAN FIND MORE INFORMATION ON UPCOMING HARLEQUIN® TITLES,
FREE EXCERPTS AND MORE AT WWW.HARLEQUIN.COM.**

HSECNM1216

*Everyone in Austin is charmed by
Keaton Whitfield Fortune, the sexy new British Fortune
in town—except Francesca Harriman, the one woman
he wants in his life! Can he win the heart of the
beautiful hometown girl?*

*Read on for a sneak preview of
A FORTUNE IN WAITING
by Michelle Major, the first book in the newest
miniseries about the Fortune clan,*
**THE FORTUNES OF TEXAS: THE SECRET
FORTUNES.**

"The dog wasn't the silver lining." He tapped one finger on the top of the box. "You and pie are the silver lining. I hope you have time to have a piece with me." He leaned in. "You know it's bad luck to eat pie alone."

She made a sound that was half laugh and half sigh. "That might explain some of the luck I've had in life. I hate to admit the amount of pie I've eaten on my own."

His heart twisted as a pain she couldn't quite hide flared in those caramel eyes. His well-honed protective streak kicked in, but it was also more than that. He wanted to take up the sword and go to battle against whatever dragons had hurt this lovely, vibrant woman.

It was an idiotic notion, both because Francesca had never given him any indication that she needed assistance slaying dragons and because he didn't have the genetic makeup of a hero. Not with Gerald Robinson as his father.

But he couldn't quite make himself walk away from the chance to give her what he could that might once again put a smile on her beautiful face.

"Then it's time for a dose of good luck." He stepped back and pulled out a chair at the small, scuffed conference table in the center of the office. "I can't think of a better way to begin than with a slice of Pick-Me-Up Pecan Pie. Join me?"

Her gaze darted to the door before settling on him. "Yes, thank you," she murmured and dropped into the seat.

Her scent drifted up to him—vanilla and spice, perfect for the type of woman who would bake a pie from scratch. He'd never considered baking to be a particularly sexy activity, but the thought of Francesca wearing an apron in the kitchen as she mixed ingredients for his pie made sparks dance across his skin.

The mental image changed to Francesca wearing nothing but an apron and—

"I have plates," he shouted and she jerked back in the chair.

"That's helpful," she answered quietly, giving him a curious look. "Do you have forks, too?"

"Yes, forks." He turned toward the small bank of cabinets installed in one corner of the trailer. "And napkins," he called over his shoulder. Damn, he sounded like a complete prat.

Don't miss
A FORTUNE IN WAITING by Michelle Major,
available January 2017 wherever
Harlequin® Special Edition books and ebooks are sold.

www.Harlequin.com

JUST CAN'T GET ENOUGH?

Join our social communities
and talk to us online.

You will have access to the latest
news on upcoming titles and special
promotions, but most importantly,
you can talk to other fans about your
favorite Harlequin reads.

Harlequin.com/Community

Facebook.com/HarlequinBooks

Twitter.com/HarlequinBooks

Pinterest.com/HarlequinBooks